THE HORROR AT CHILLER HOUSE

GOOSEBUMPS HorrorLand™

#1 REVENGE OF THE LIVING DUMMY
#2 CREEP FROM THE DEEP
#3 MONSTER BLOOD FOR BREAKFAST!
#4 THE SCREAM OF THE HAUNTED MASK
#5 DR. MANIAC VS. ROBBY SCHWARTZ
#6 WHO'S YOUR MUMMY?
#7 MY FRIENDS CALL ME MONSTER
#8 SAY CHEESE — AND DIE SCREAMING!
#9 WELCOME TO CAMP SLITHER
#10 HELP! WE HAVE STRANGE POWERS!
#11 ESCAPE FROM HORRORLAND
#12 THE STREETS OF PANIC PARK
#13 WHEN THE GHOST DOG HOWLS
#14 LITTLE SHOP OF HAMSTERS
#15 HEADS, YOU LOSE!
#16 SPECIAL EDITION: WEIRDO HALLOWEEN
#17 THE WIZARD OF OOZE
#18 SLAPPY NEW YEAR!
#19 THE HORROR AT CHILLER HOUSE

GOOSEBUMPS® MOST WANTED

#1 PLANET OF THE LAWN GNOMES
#2 SON OF SLAPPY
#3 HOW I MET MY MONSTER
#4 FRANKENSTEIN'S DOG
#5 DR. MANIAC WILL SEE YOU NOW
#6 CREATURE TEACHER: FINAL EXAM
#7 A NIGHTMARE ON CLOWN STREET

SPECIAL EDITION #1 ZOMBIE HALLOWEEN
SPECIAL EDITION #2 THE 12 SCREAMS OF CHRISTMAS
SPECIAL EDITION #3 TRICK OR TRAP

GOOSEBUMPS®

Also available as ebooks

NIGHT OF THE LIVING DUMMY
DEEP TROUBLE
MONSTER BLOOD
THE HAUNTED MASK
ONE DAY AT HORRORLAND
THE CURSE OF THE MUMMY'S TOMB
BE CAREFUL WHAT YOU WISH FOR
SAY CHEESE AND DIE!
THE HORROR AT CAMP JELLYJAM
HOW I GOT MY SHRUNKEN HEAD
THE WEREWOLF OF FEVER SWAMP
A NIGHT IN TERROR TOWER
WELCOME TO DEAD HOUSE
WELCOME TO CAMP NIGHTMARE
GHOST BEACH
THE SCARECROW WALKS AT MIDNIGHT
YOU CAN'T SCARE ME!
RETURN OF THE MUMMY
REVENGE OF THE LAWN GNOMES
PHANTOM OF THE AUDITORIUM
VAMPIRE BREATH
STAY OUT OF THE BASEMENT
A SHOCKER ON SHOCK STREET
LET'S GET INVISIBLE!
NIGHT OF THE LIVING DUMMY 2
NIGHT OF THE LIVING DUMMY 3
THE ABOMINABLE SNOWMAN OF PASADENA
THE BLOB THAT ATE EVERYONE
THE GHOST NEXT DOOR
THE HAUNTED CAR
ATTACK OF THE GRAVEYARD GHOULS
PLEASE DON'T FEED THE VAMPIRE

ALSO AVAILABLE:

IT CAME FROM OHIO!: MY LIFE AS A WRITER by R.L. Stine

THE HORROR AT CHILLER HOUSE

R.L. STINE

SCHOLASTIC INC.
New York Toronto London Auckland
Sydney Mexico City New Delhi Hong Kong

ISBN: 978-0-545-16200-5

Goosebumps book series created by Parachute Press, Inc.

12 11 10 9 8 15 16/0

Printed in the U.S.A. 40
First printing, January 2011

MEET JONATHAN CHILLER . . .

He owns Chiller House, the HorrorLand gift shop. Sometimes Chiller refused to let kids pay for their gifts. He said, "You can pay me *next time*."

What did he mean by that?

You're about to find out.

Because *next time* has arrived!

Six kids find themselves pulled from their homes, back to Chiller's frightening shop. "It's payback time," Chiller tells them. "We're going to play a game."

The kids quickly discover his game may have *no winners*.

They have no choice. They must play to survive. They are trapped in the most terrifying HorrorLand adventure of them all!

PART ONE

1960

1

He didn't want to do his homework. He hated the big science and math textbooks. Sometimes he thought about ripping out each page. Every one of them, one by one. He wanted to rip them out and crinkle them up and toss them into the fireplace.

He'd be so happy watching them smoke and burn.

Except he didn't have a fireplace in his bedroom. His walls were filled with bookshelves. That's where he kept all his board games, and puppets, and action figures, and toy soldiers, and costumes. Everything was all jammed together, as if he were living in a big closet.

Maybe that's why he spent so much time gazing out the window. His one window that looked out on his backyard.

The grass was tall in the back. There were a few low evergreen bushes. And his mother had a small vegetable garden behind the wooden shed. That was all. The yard was pretty bare.

No swing set or lawn furniture. No patio. No place to sit in the sun or play. Well, his parents didn't like him to play outside. And they definitely didn't like it when he sneaked out the back door and took himself for a walk in the woods.

The backyard ended at the woods. So it was a short walk to the tall, tangled trees, the cool darkness, the tangy, piney smells, the crunch of dead brown leaves under his shoes.

He liked to hide back there and pretend he was an explorer in a new country. You might guess that he had a good imagination — and you'd be right.

He imagined that no one had ever walked there before. He was the first. He was discovering new lands and claiming them for himself.

He battled the wild woods people. He defeated them. He *destroyed* them. Then he moved on to discover even more lands.

He had to sneak out to do his exploring. Mother and Father said it was dangerous in the woods. His father wouldn't go there without his hunting crossbow. Mother forbade him to go past the backyard.

That's why he gazed out the window so often. Right now, two shiny black crows were fighting over a worm in the grass. He liked to watch them fight. The way they flapped their wings so furiously and pecked at each other.

He liked to see them peck and peck and peck, till the feathers flew and blood spattered all over the grass.

Sometimes he imagined he saw kids in the backyard at the edge of the woods. Kids his age who were coming to visit him. He imagined they were his good friends, and they were coming to play games, and watch him do a puppet show, and share secrets, and have bowls of popcorn with him.

He wanted to be a normal ten-year-old. He *thought* he could be a normal ten-year-old.

He'd love to go to school and have friends and go to birthday parties and sleepovers. But Mother said he was better than that. She said he had a special brain that must be nurtured.

He didn't really know what *nurtured* meant. And he refused to look it up in the fat dictionary they made him keep on the corner of his big mahogany desk.

If he had a special brain, he didn't want it. He'd give it back. He'd trade it for a normal brain. No joke.

Sometimes he played a game he invented called *The Brain Game*. He asked himself really hard questions and then made up really stupid answers. He didn't know why, but he thought it was very funny. His stupid answers always cracked him up.

He liked to make up games. And he liked to put on plays with his toy soldiers and spacemen. That was normal — right?

Wow. Those two crows were really having a battle. They were shrieking and cawing their heads off. They made such a racket, he didn't hear his bedroom door open. And he didn't hear his mother walk into the room.

"Why aren't you studying?"

Her voice made him jump. He nearly banged his head on the window.

His mother had a big, powerful voice. She never whispered.

Everything about her was big. She was tall, taller than his father. She had broad shoulders and big hands, and she walked heavily, as if she was wearing boots even when she wasn't.

He thought she was kind of pretty. Her eyes were steely gray, and she had a cold stare. But her wavy blond hair was nice. And when she smiled, her whole face crinkled up, the only time she looked gentle.

He turned away from the window to face her. "Just taking a break," he said.

He got the cold, silvery stare. "I heard you playing a game before. You are wasting your good brain. Get to your studies."

She pointed to the stack of textbooks on his desk. "The great scientists await," she said.

Let them wait! he thought.

But he said, “Okay.” And he shuffled over to the desk. He slid into his big black leather desk chair and opened a science book.

She stood there watching him, her arms crossed in front of her white sweater. He pretended to read. He suddenly had an idea for a new puppet show. Two puppets fighting to the death.

“Every day you need to expand your brain,” Mother said. “Every day your brain will grow bigger.”

That made him snicker. It sounded like a horror movie. *The Brain That Wouldn’t Stop Growing.*

He wasn’t allowed to watch horror movies. But he read about them.

Finally, Mother strode to the door. She closed it behind her.

As soon as she was gone, he stood up and walked over to his puppet shelf. He had marionettes and hand puppets. And a set of finger puppets his grandmother sent him when he was six.

It was a very good puppet collection. He liked to collect things. It made him feel like his room was crowded. And then he wasn’t so lonely.

He picked up his sad-clown puppet. It had a bright red-and-white-striped costume with a red ruffle around its neck. But it had the saddest frown on its face and little teardrops under its eyes. He named the puppet Droopy.

He carried Droopy to his desk and made him sit next to his science textbook. "We'll read it together," he told him. "That's what friends do. They share things."

He started to read. But voices outside his bedroom door made him stop and look up.

Mother and Father were in the hall. They were arguing. This happened a lot.

They were talking in hushed whispers. They didn't want him to hear. But the whispers were loud enough. He could hear every word.

"Why don't you let him be normal?" Father demanded.

Mother didn't reply. So Father continued. "You are turning my son into a freak."

"He's *our* son," Mother said.

"I don't care. I don't like what you are doing to him. You have to let him go to school and be with other kids."

"He's not like other kids," Mother insisted.

He'd heard her say this so many times. He imagined himself grabbing her arms and shaking her . . . shaking her and saying, "Yes, I am. Yes, I *am* like other kids."

The crows finally stopped cawing. He could hear his parents' hushed voices so clearly now.

"He is too smart for the other kids," Mother said. "He has to study. He has to use his brilliant mind."

“You’re ruining him,” Father told her. Even through the thick door, he could hear the anger in Father’s voice. He pictured his face, hard and tight and red. “You’re turning him into a freak. He’s a weird little freak.”

A door slammed.

He jumped to his feet. He let out a hoarse cry of anger. “No, I’m NOT!” he screamed at the door. “I’m NOT a freak! NOT a freak!”

He grabbed Droopy. He squeezed his cloth body hard with one hand — and ripped off one of his arms.

“Not a freak! Not a freak!”

He tore off Droopy’s head and tossed it in the trash basket. He tore off a leg. Then another arm. Pulling and tearing and screaming. He ripped the striped costume to shreds.

His chest was heaving. He couldn’t catch his breath. He ripped and clawed at the puppet.

It felt good. It really did.

War on the Red Planet!

He lined his spacemen up, ready for battle. This was the biggest war the planet Mars had ever seen.

He collected monster figures, too. He had some of the most popular ones from TV. Billy Bigfoot. And The Creature from the Bottomless Sewer. And Abominable Two-Headed Spider Boy.

He wasn't allowed to watch TV. But he read about all the monster movies and shows.

He pretended the monsters were the Martians. His silver space cadets were the good guys. Their ray guns could blast a Martian to molecules.

He made all the sound effects with his mouth. Explosions. The *zip zip zip* of ray guns. Martians screaming as they fell.

It was a few days after he ripped Droopy the Clown to pieces. He missed Droopy. He was an important part of his puppet collection. When he tore him up, he didn't even realize it. It was scary to be that angry and not even know what he was doing.

That morning before the war on Mars, he worked on his stamp collection. And he organized his antique bottle collection on its shelf.

He was doing anything he could to keep away from the chapter entitled "The Physics of the Gravitational Pull" he was supposed to be reading in his science book.

Last night, Mother made him read his history text till bedtime. When he looked in the mirror this morning, his eyes were tired and bloodshot.

KABOOOOOM.

He dropped a pillow over the Martian monsters. They crumbled beneath it. The war was brutal.

But he stopped the battle when once again he heard his parents arguing outside his door. His father sounded very angry this time. His mother was not arguing back.

"Listen to him in there," Father said. "All he does is make up baby games and play with toys. He lives in a fantasy world."

"I keep telling him to study harder," Mother said. "What else can I do?"

"You won't let him be normal," Father boomed. "It's enough. Enough! I'm going to make a man out of him!"

The spaceman figure dropped from his hand. He shoved the monsters off the bed and climbed to his feet.

He heard Father's heavy footsteps treading toward his room.

And he heard Mother's frightened voice: "Charles — stop. What are you going to do?"

The bedroom door swung open. He felt a shock of fear as Father came bursting in.

Father wasn't tall but he was built like a bear, big and athletic, broad and tough looking. He was red-faced and stubbly. He didn't like to shave. He had straight black hair cut in a short flattop. His eyes were pale blue, under thick black eyebrows. He had a stare like a ray gun beam.

He wore flannel shirts and baggy jeans that he seldom had cleaned. He laughed sometimes, big he-man, cruel laughter. But he seldom smiled.

Father turned his blue eyes on the monsters and spacemen scattered on the bedroom floor. Then he raised his gaze. He scratched his stubbly beard and stared hard.

"There are wild turkeys in the woods," he said. He didn't talk — he boomed.

The boy didn't know how to reply to Father. He just stared back at him, his legs trembling.

"You want to come hunting with me?" Father demanded.

The boy swallowed. His mouth suddenly felt so dry.

He pictured the big crossbows his father kept in the mudroom at the back of the house. The boy liked to fight *pretend* wars. But those crossbows frightened him a lot.

Father didn't believe in using a hunting rifle. He said rifles made it too easy. Hunting with a crossbow required skill.

The boy shuddered every time he walked past the weapons case.

The crossbows terrified him.

Father narrowed his eyes at the boy. "Do you want to come hunting or not?"

No. No way. He didn't want to go.

But he wanted Father to like him. He had to show his father that he wasn't a cowardly baby and a freak.

"Yes," he said. His voice cracked just a little. "Yes. Okay. Let's go."

Clouds covered the sun, and the woods grew dark. It was early spring, and the air still carried a chill. It had rained the day before, and the ground was soft and muddy.

His shoes sank into the mud as he hurried to keep up with Father. Father took long strides, crunching the twigs and leaves under his boots.

He had the crossbow slung over the right shoulder of his brown leather jacket. A quiver of arrows bounced on his back.

The boy heard the trees shaking overhead. Birds probably, lighting in the branches.

Something scampered across their path. A fat brown squirrel.

"The turkeys were on the other side of that clearing," his father whispered. He pointed. "Two families of them. Some fat, juicy birds. They travel together in a line."

His words made the boy excited. He guessed because Father was actually talking to him, explaining something to him.

He usually only grunted a few words. Or shouted at the boy about something he had done wrong.

This was the first time *ever* that the two were on an adventure together — like friends, almost.

So the boy was excited — but also frightened. Watching that deadly crossbow made him feel shaky and afraid.

And as they walked, he kept his eyes on it. He watched it bob up and down over his father's shoulder.

And he thought about what a powerful weapon it was. How fast and straight it sent the arrows flying.

He imagined the *thwocccck* the arrow made, driven deep into a tree trunk.

He had watched Father practice target shooting for hours in the back of their house. It never failed to fill him with cold dread.

The sky brightened a little. Some light washed down through the thick trees overhead. A gust of wind made the branches tremble and creak.

Father kicked a rock out of his way. It made a loud *thump* as it slammed into a tree trunk, then bounced aside.

The boy slipped over a thicket of wet leaves and fell to his knees. His father didn't notice. He just kept taking those long strides. The boy scrambled to catch up to him.

"Father —" he started.

He raised a hand to shush the boy. He led the way into a small grassy clearing. He pressed a finger against his lips, then pointed.

The boy saw four or five fat wild turkeys, heads bobbing as they walked. "There they are," Father whispered.

Then, to the boy's surprise, Father slid the crossbow off his shoulder and shoved it hard into his hands. The boy wasn't expecting it. He nearly dropped it.

He could feel his heart thudding in his chest. He felt a little dizzy. The crossbow was heavier than he imagined.

"But, Father —" he started.

Father had his eyes on the bobbing, strutting turkeys.

"Let's see you give it a try, son," he whispered. "Hurry. Hold it steady like this."

"But, Father —"

He moved the boy's hands over the handle. He pulled an arrow from the quiver and fit it into the crossbow.

"I'll steady it for you, son," he said softly. "Hold it here." He moved the boy's hand down to the trigger. "Aim through the sight."

The boy struggled to hold it up. It was heavy — and too long for him. He couldn't balance it. He didn't know how to aim or keep it steady.

"I — I'm just a kid, Father," he stammered. "I'm only ten. This thing is too big for me." He didn't mean for it to come out so whiny. "Look. It's almost as long as I am."

Father made a disgusted face. His blue eyes turned cold. "You've got to learn sometime," he said through his clenched teeth.

The boy didn't want him to be angry. He wanted desperately to make his father proud of him. "Okay," he said. "I'll try."

"Be a man," he said. "A man has to know how to hunt."

He raised the crossbow to his shoulder. His knees started to fold. He almost sank to the ground. He just couldn't balance it.

"Hold it like this," Father said. He moved the handle over the boy's shoulder. Then he slid his son's hand to the trigger.

Across the clearing, two more wild turkeys appeared. They began to peck at something in the grass. There were at least seven or eight of them now.

"I — I don't really know how to aim," the boy said.

"Don't worry about that," Father replied. "Just get the feel of the crossbow. You don't have to shoot any turkeys today. First you have to learn to handle the weapon."

The boy nodded. His heart was still racing. But he felt a little better. At least his father didn't really expect him to shoot anything.

"Take a practice shot," Father said. He turned his son slightly and pointed. "Just aim at those trees. Go ahead. Take a shot. You'll get the feel of it."

Could the boy do it?

He suddenly felt terrified. His hands were so sweaty, the crossbow handle felt slippery. He was trembling so hard. He wondered if Father could see him shaking.

I want him to be proud of me, the boy thought. *I want him to like me.*

I really don't want to fail.

He took a deep breath and let it out. He tightened both hands. Aimed through the sight.

He aimed the sleek, deadly arrow at a fat tree trunk across the grass.

He took another shuddering breath. Squeezed the trigger with all his strength. Fired.

And as burning pain shot through his body, he opened his mouth in a deafening scream.

4

What have I done?

The pain throbbed . . . throbbed . . . blinding pain . . .

It faded slowly. And slowly, the boy's senses began to snap back. His brain started up again.

He saw the crossbow, still in his hands. No arrow. He had shot the arrow.

Above him, the trees appeared to tilt and sway. The whole earth was trembling. All a blur.

His father's scream snapped him alert: "You shot yourself in the foot! I don't believe it! You shot your own foot!"

"Ohhh." A groan escaped the boy's throat.

He glanced down and saw the shaft of the arrow poking straight up through the top of his left shoe. His foot throbbed in pain, and the pain shot up his leg, his whole body.

"I don't believe it. I don't believe it," Father repeated, shaking his head.

He started to laugh. He laughed so hard, tears ran down his cheeks.

Father laughed till he could barely breathe.

Father gave the arrow a hard pull and jerked it from his son's foot. Bright red blood spurted over the boy's shoe.

At home, Mother dabbed the wound with alcohol. She wrapped the foot gently in a long white bandage.

Father stood against the bathroom wall, watching. He rubbed his stubbled cheeks but didn't say a word.

Later, the boy was in his bedroom, lying on his back on the bed. He shut his eyes. He tried to calm down, tried to get his heart to stop racing.

If only his bandaged foot would stop aching and throbbing.

He kept picturing the fat turkeys, their heads bobbing as if they were listening to music. And the tall trees spinning, trembling over his head as he tried to balance that crossbow.

Father's voice interrupted his thoughts. His parents were in the hall again. They didn't know their son could hear every word.

"Okay, you win," Father said. "Let Jonny stay in his room with his toys and his books."

"That's where he belongs," Mother replied. The boy could hear the anger in her voice. "He's a brilliant boy. You had no business taking Jonny hunting with you. No business at all."

"Don't worry," Father said. "I *never* will take him again!"

Those words made Jonny sit straight up. Anger swept over him. Anger so powerful it made him forget his aching, pulsing pain.

"I'll show you, Father!" he shouted at the bedroom door. "One day, I'll show you that I can be a man. One day, you'll be *proud* that I am your son!"

He stomped across the room to his book-shelves. He grabbed up spacemen and cowboys and monsters and soldiers. He gathered them into his arms. Then he lined them all up. One by one, he lined them up on the floor in front of him.

He went to the closet. He pulled out his red bathrobe. He wrapped the robe around him.

Then he stepped back to the figures on the floor. His subjects. His loyal subjects.

He raised his arms in the royal red robe. And he shouted: "I am JONATHAN CHILLER, your king! I am all-powerful. You will obey me. You will all obey me!"

PART TWO

TODAY

5

"Whoa." I uttered a startled cry.

White light quivered all around me, so bright I still saw it when I shut my eyes.

Slowly, the light faded. I blinked a few times. I shook my head. Ran my hand through my blond hair.

Sometimes you see funny videos of people spinning around inside big clothes dryers. That's what I thought of. That's what I felt like.

Like I'd been spinning endlessly in burning hot air.

And now the room started to come into focus. I saw cluttered shelves and tall display cases. A grinning skeleton propped against the back door.

I knew where I was. This was the little souvenir store where I bought that evil dummy, Slappy. I was back in Chiller House. Back in HorrorLand.

But — how?

I shook myself hard, as if trying to wake from a dream. *Am I going crazy?*

That thought flashed through my spinning brain.

I reviewed the facts. I had to make everything clear.

My name. It's Ray Gordon. I'm twelve. My little brother's name is Brandon. I shouldn't call him *little* brother. He's twice my size.

Okay. My memory was fine. My brain wasn't totally playing jokes on me.

But one minute I had been at home in my room. And now here I stood, in the aisle of this little shop in HorrorLand.

And as the bright light faded and my mind cleared, I realized I wasn't alone. I saw other kids about my age huddled together at the front of the store. I counted them. Five in all. Three boys and two girls.

They all stared at me, as if they'd been waiting for me. But their faces were filled with surprise.

I took a few shaky steps toward them. "Are you — are you surprised to be here, too?" I stammered.

They all began talking at once. I could tell they were as confused as me. Confused and frightened.

I gazed around. The six of us were alone in the store. Where was Jonathan Chiller, the old guy who owned the place?

I suddenly remembered. "I held a tiny Horror in my hand," I said. "It was glowing. Green and yellow light came out of it, and it pulled me . . ."

"Me, too," the girl with curly red hair said.

"The little Horrors brought us here somehow," a round-faced boy, built like a middle linebacker, chimed in.

"Were you all here in this store before?" I asked.

Everyone nodded and said yes.

"Did you all take something home from here?" I asked.

Again, the answer was yes.

"I picked a joke coin," the very tall girl with straight brown hair and shiny blue eyes said. "A two-headed coin. It got me in all kinds of trouble."

That started everyone talking again.

"I bought a leather cord with an ancient dog tooth on it," the big, round-faced boy said.

"I brought home Insta-Gro Pets that grew gigantic!"

Everyone had a crazy story. I think I had the craziest of all. Who would believe a wooden ventriloquist's dummy could come to life?

As we all shared our stories of horror, I began to catch their names. The middle linebacker with the very worried expression was Andy. The way-tall girl was Jessica. The other girl, the one with red hair, was Meg.

Marco was the one who talked about comic books and some superhero character named The Ooze. Marco was tall and dark and serious looking.

The other boy was Sam. He was short and smaller than the rest of us. He had black hair and dark eyes. His two front teeth poked out when he talked, like Bugs Bunny teeth.

It didn't take long to put the stories together. All six of us had bought gifts or souvenirs here. All six of us had scary adventures, mostly because of those souvenirs.

"The old dude, Jonathan Chiller, gave me a little Horror," Sam said. "He told me to take a little Horror home with me."

"Me, too!" several kids cried.

We all started talking again. It turned out that Chiller didn't let any of us pay for our gifts. He said we could pay him *next time.*

I felt a chill run slowly down my back. I suddenly felt cold all over.

Is this it? Is this payback time?

6

The shelves and cases were jammed with items. Big stuffed monsters had tumbled out into the aisle. I saw a headless monkey with a lightbulb where its head should be.

Grinning, prune-wrinkled shrunken heads dangled on rubber cords from the ceiling. Globs of rubber vomit glistened wetly on a low shelf. One glass case was jammed full with ugly plastic cockroaches.

The stuff all seemed really funny the first time I was here with my brother. But now it was just frightening.

"How do we get home?" Meg asked. "My parents must be frantic."

"Does anyone have a phone?" I asked.

Sam pulled a cell phone from his jeans pocket. He peered at the screen. He pushed the power button. He shook the phone.

Then he let out a sigh. "Totally dead. I don't

get it. I just recharged it before . . . before I was brought here."

No one else had a phone with them. We had all been pulled away from our homes without any warning.

"Where is Chiller?" I said. "We have a lot of questions for him."

I made my way to the back room. The door had a werewolf poster across it. It swung open easily. I poked my head inside.

A tiny supply room. More shelves of weird stuff. But no sign of the old shop owner.

We all walked up and down the aisles. He wasn't hiding anywhere in the store.

"This is kind of like a comic book story," Marco said. "You know. Time travel. No, not time travel. But some kind of travel. There was an Ooze story about a bunch of kids who could jump from one place to another."

"But this isn't a comic book," Meg said, shaking her head. "This is our *lives*."

I stepped behind the front desk. The screen saver was on the computer monitor. It showed skeleton fish swimming in black water.

I saw a stack of papers in the corner of the desk. I picked them up.

"Hey. This is *disturbing*," I said.

I held up the stack. They were photographs. I turned them around and shuffled through them. Grainy, blurred black-and-white photos.

“That’s *us*!” Sam said. He grabbed some of the photos from my hand and studied them. “Photos taken of each of us in this store.”

Jessica pointed up to the ceiling. We all saw the small black security camera up there. It was aimed down at the front desk.

“Chiller took our picture when we stood here,” Sam said.

I took the photos back from him. My picture was on the top. I gazed at it — and felt a chill.

“Look,” I said. I held it up so everyone could see it. “Someone has added something to it.”

Yes. Someone had taken a black marker. They drew an arrow through my head.

I shuffled through the stack. Jessica’s picture had an arrow drawn through her head, too. And Meg’s. And Andy’s.

“All of them,” I said. “Did Chiller do this? Someone very carefully drew an arrow through our heads.”

“Creepy,” Andy muttered. “What does it mean? Is it some kind of sick threat?”

I heard a loud cough. We all turned toward the front door.

Jonathan Chiller stood in the doorway. Blue light from the front window poured over him, making him look ghostlike.

“Welcome back,” he said, and a cold smile spread slowly over his face.

Chiller stood in the eerie blue light, hands in the pockets of his old-fashioned vest. The light gleamed off his square eyeglasses perched on the end of his long nose.

His thinning hair was tied behind his head. His ruffled shirt and high-collared suit looked like they came from a museum. He reminded me of Ben Franklin, or maybe the old guy on the oatmeal box.

We didn't wait for him to come closer. We rushed toward him, bombarding him with questions.

"Why did you bring us back here?"

"Why did you take our pictures?"

"What do you want? How could you do this?"

"Why did you draw arrows through our heads? Have you *kidnapped* us?"

"Send us back home — now!"

His smile didn't fade as we pushed up close.

His tiny eyes flashed behind the square glasses. He waved his hands to quiet us down.

"So glad to see you all back in my shop," he said in his croaky old voice. He rubbed his hands together. "Now my game can begin."

"Game?" I cried. "What kind of game?"

He stepped forward, his big stomach leading the way. He left the blue light behind him. The skin on his face was pale and flabby. His boots trod heavily on the wood floor.

He took the little Horror from my hand. I didn't realize I was still holding it.

"Now, I believe I have collected all your little Horrors," he said. He tossed the Horror into a trash basket under the front counter. "Those old ones are worthless. They can't be reused."

"Are you going to send us home?" Jessica demanded. She had a big, angry voice. Her blue eyes locked on Chiller.

"Of course I'll send you home," Chiller said softly. The thin smile returned to his face. "After we play our game."

"You brought us all back here to play a game?" I demanded.

He took the stack of photographs and straightened them. "Do you remember your *first* visits here?" he asked. "You all bought souvenirs? Jessica, you bought that two-headed coin? Sam, you bought the Insta-Gro Pets?"

"Yes, we remember," Jessica said, rolling her eyes. "What about them?"

Chiller set the photographs down in a perfectly straight pile. He gazed from one face to the next. "Maybe you also remember that you didn't pay for your gifts?"

We all muttered replies.

His smile revealed a gleaming gold tooth. "Guess what, kids. It's *payback time*."

"You — you planned this all along?" I stammered. "From our first visit here. You deliberately didn't let us pay — because you *knew* you were going to bring us back here?"

He ignored my question. He clasped his pale hands together. "I love games — don't you?" he said. "I don't know why you are so angry. I think you'll enjoy my game. I think you'll find it . . . challenging."

Silence for a moment.

I guess we were all thinking hard about what he was saying.

Finally, Jessica spoke up. "What if we don't want to play?"

Chiller's smile faded. His expression grew cold. "You *do* want to go home again — don't you?"

8

I felt a wave of fear sweep over me. I took a step back from the front counter.

Chiller wasn't smiling that sick smile anymore. His eyes grew icy behind the old glasses. He grasped the end of the counter with both hands and studied us.

"Now, get those worried looks off your faces," he said. "I'm sure you will be very successful at my game. I know you will all be winners."

"And go home?" Sam asked.

Chiller nodded. "Yes. Winners go home."

What does THAT mean? Does he mean ONLY winners go home?

He reached under the counter and pulled out a small red chest. He lifted the lid and pulled out a little green-and-purple Horror doll. It looked exactly like the big Horrors who work in the park in all the shops and restaurants, run the games and rides, and act as guides.

"You all took a little Horror home with you," he said. "Now you will need to find one of these Horrors to take you back home."

"Why are you talking in riddles?" I asked. "What do you want us to do?"

Chiller studied the little Horror doll. "I love riddles — don't you?" he asked. He thumped the countertop with his fingers. "Here's a riddle for you. See if you can get it. What did the spider say to the fly?"

We all stared at him in silence.

Did he really steal us from our homes, transport us here against our will to ask us *riddles*?

"What did the spider say to the fly?" Chiller repeated. "Anyone?"

No one spoke.

"Okay, I'll tell you. The spider didn't say *anything* to the fly. The spider bit the fly's *head* off!"

Chiller tossed back his head and laughed like a maniac. He thumped the counter with both hands and laughed till tears ran down his sagging cheeks.

Marco leaned close to me. "He's totally nuts," he whispered.

I nodded.

Yes. Chiller seemed to be totally nuts. And we were trapped here with him.

He finally stopped laughing. He pulled a lacy handkerchief from his pants pocket, wiped his wet cheeks, then blew his nose loudly. As he tucked the handkerchief back in his pocket, his expression turned serious.

"Let me explain my little scavenger hunt," he said. "It's quite simple. I've hidden six of these little Horrors around HorrorLand. One for each of you. They are just like the Horrors that brought you here. I placed them inside six little treasure chests like this one. You see —"

"This is a *huge* park," Jessica interrupted, tossing back her long brown hair. "How are we supposed to find tiny chests —"

"Look at it. It's bright red," Chiller said. "How easy is that? When you find a chest, take out the little Horror. Squeeze it between your hands, and it will take you home."

Andy shook his head, frowning unhappily. "What if we don't play your game? You have to send us home. You can't keep us here."

Chiller peered at him through the small eyeglasses. "I think you should play the game, Andy. Your parents don't know you are here. No one knows where you are. The quickest way to get home is to find one of the Horrors."

I turned and gazed out the glass front door. I saw dozens of people crossing Zombie Plaza, the main square of HorrorLand. The shops and restaurants were clearing out. It was almost closing time. People were heading to the exit gate.

"This park covers acres and acres," I said. "No way can we find six little chests here. It's impossible."

Chiller reached across the counter and patted my shoulder. "I don't want my game to be too hard. How much fun is that? I'm going to give you some help, Ray."

He reached under the counter and pulled out a stack of cards. They looked like trading cards. I saw strange faces on them.

"Here. Take a card," he said.

He shoved a card into my hand. Then he handed a card to each of the other five kids.

"These are *Helper* cards," he said. "See the face on your card? That person will be your Helper. The Helpers know where the chests are hidden, and they will help you find them."

I gazed at my card. A fat, sweaty man in a floppy white chef's hat. His name was at the bottom in bold black type: CHEF BELCHER.

I glanced at some of the other cards. MURDER THE CLOWN. MONDO THE MAGICAL. MADAME DOOM.

"Find the person on your card," Chiller said. "Show them the card. Then they will know you are playing the game. They will help you and give you important clues."

"How do we know we can trust you?" Marco demanded.

Chiller snickered. "Do you have a choice?"

I stared at my Helper card. Was there really a Chef Belcher? Did these helpers know where the chests were hidden? Or was Chiller just messing with us?

Meg asked the question that was running through all of our minds. "If we find a little Horror, will you really let us go home?"

Chiller's cheeks turned pink. He narrowed his eyes at Meg. "I sent you home the last time — didn't I? Do you think I'm a cheater?"

He waved us toward the door with both hands. "Go. The game starts *now*. Go find your Helpers. Find the red chests. Good luck."

Marco grumbled something under his breath. Beside him, Andy looked pale and frightened. The two girls walked together as we started for the door.

Sam and I bumped as we both reached for the doorknob. I pushed the door open and took one step outside.

"Oh, wait. Come back," Chiller called.

We all turned back.

"Wait," he said. "I almost forgot. I forgot to tell you the *dangerous* part."

We shuffled back to the front counter. I had a fluttery feeling in my chest. I get that when I'm scared or nervous.

What did he mean by *dangerous*?

"I can't believe I forgot the best part," Chiller said. His little eyes flashed. He bent down and picked something up from behind the counter.

A few kids gasped when they saw it. A crossbow.

"You see," Chiller said, "some of my friends and I are having a hunting party."

He fumbled in his drawer and pulled out a feathered arrow with a long shaft. "And guess what we're hunting, kids? We're hunting YOU."

"Whoa! Wait a minute!"

"You're joking — right?"

"No way! This can't be real!"

We all started shouting at once.

I had my eyes on the arrow as he carefully fitted it into the crossbow.

"Hunting you will add a lot of excitement to the game," he said. "While you hunt for the red treasure chests, we hunt for *you*!"

We were all shouting and asking questions.

I don't think he heard us. His eyes looked hazy. He seemed to be in his own world.

"Father never thought I was a good hunter," he said. "I wish he were here to see how skilled I have become."

He raised the crossbow. Aimed it over our heads at the back wall of the shop.

A target hung on the wall between the two rows of shelves.

Chiller narrowed his eyes. Aimed carefully — and fired.

The arrow bounced off the wall. It missed the target by at least three feet.

"Uh-oh," Chiller muttered. "This could get *messy*."

He blinked when he turned back to us. I think he'd forgotten we were there. He gripped the crossbow tightly in one hand.

"This is a joke — right? You can't really hunt us," I said. "Those arrows aren't real — right?"

He shrugged the shoulders of his old-fashioned jacket. "It's a game. Just a game," he muttered. "We all love games, right? Have fun with it. And . . . if you play well, you won't get hurt."

What does THAT mean?

Chiller pulled another arrow from the drawer. "My friends and I are giving you a head start," he said. "We won't come after you till tomorrow morning. Or is it tonight? I forget."

He frowned and shook his head. "You'd better stay alert."

Again, we all started shouting and protesting.

"Get going!" Chiller shouted over our cries. "You're wasting time. The game has started." He waved us to the door again.

"What about the real Horrors?" I demanded. "All the park workers. Do they know about your game?"

"Of course not," Chiller replied. "I don't think they'd approve."

"So what if we *tell* them?" I asked.

That made Chiller laugh. "Do you really think they'll believe such a crazy story?"

"You — you're not joking?" Andy stammered. "You and your friends are really going to *hunt* us?"

Chiller didn't answer. Instead, he raised the crossbow — and sent another arrow flying toward the wall target.

This one went so wild, it hit the ceiling and stuck there.

I stared up at it. The arrow had a suction cup at the end.

I breathed a sigh of relief. He was trying to scare us, but he wasn't using real arrows.

"Come on, let's go," Marco said. He trotted to the door. "We've got to get away from here."

We stampeded out of the store. I was the last to leave. I turned at the doorway.

Behind the counter, Chiller had that same foggy look on his face. He was talking, even though he was all alone.

I didn't really understand what he was saying.

"I'm a hunter, Daddy," he said. "See? I'm a hunter — just like you wanted."

PART THREE

10

We ran out onto the plaza. It was a warm night. The air smelled of popcorn and cotton candy. A tiny sliver of a moon hung low in the sky.

Lights were flickering out. The park was closing. People were hurrying to the exit gates.

We ran together, dodging baby strollers, families, and groups of teenagers.

Finally, we came to a stop beside the front wall of the hotel, the Stagger Inn. I turned back toward the plaza. I couldn't see the Chiller House shop from there. Somehow, that made me feel a little better.

We leaned against the stone wall of the hotel and struggled to catch our breath. A Horror passed by pushing a purple food cart. "Chicken heads on a stick!" he shouted. "I have a few stale ones left. How about it? Crunchy chicken heads on a stick. It tastes better than it sounds."

I don't think any of us were hungry.

Meg shook out her curly red hair. She stepped away from the wall. "Listen, guys," she said, "this isn't as bad as it sounds."

"Yeah. At least the arrows aren't real," I said. "That's the good news — right? And the bad news —"

"Even if we find the red chests, we don't know if Chiller will really let us go home," Marco said. "That's the bad news."

"He did this to me before," Meg said. "Last Halloween he brought me here. He made me play a different game. A crazy game. I had to prove to him that I was *me*!"

"Oh, wow!" Jessica shook her head. "He brought you back here *twice*?"

"Yes," Meg replied. "Last time, I was terrified. Scared out of my mind. But in the end, I held one of those little Horrors. And it sent me home."

"I don't care," I said. "I don't like this game. *No way* I trust Chiller. I just want to get out of this park, as far away from that crazy old guy as I can get."

"You can't trust him," Andy said. "Like I told you, he gave me a cord with an old dog tooth on it. He said it was a Wishing Tooth. And guess what? When I wished on it, this zombie dog came back to life, searching for its tooth!"

"He sold me these Insta-Gro Pets," Sam said. "And when I got home, I was attacked by vicious hamsters."

"Hamsters?" Jessica cried. "Vicious *hamsters*?!"

We all burst out laughing.

Sam blushed. "It's not funny," he muttered. "Hamsters have teeth, you know."

That made us laugh again.

"I could tell you an even weirder story," Marco said. "How I met The Ooze and had to fight these supervillains. It was totally insane."

"Enough stories," I said. "I guess we all have crazy stories, thanks to Chiller." I pointed. "There's the exit gate. Duh. Why don't we just walk out of here?"

"Yeah, why not?" Sam agreed. "Look at all the people leaving. We'll just walk out with them."

"Then we can find someone with a phone that works," Jessica said. "And call for help. No problem."

I watched people walking easily through the turnstiles. "Piece of cake," I said. "Let's go."

Had Chiller forgotten that we could just walk away from his crazy game?

I took off, jogging toward the gate. I had that fluttery feeling in my chest again. This time, I knew it was just excitement about escaping.

The others came trotting behind me. No one spoke. We were all eager to get to the other side of the gate, into the parking lot, where we could get help.

I reached the exit first. I took a deep breath. Walked slowly. Tried to look calm.

I stepped up behind a family with two little kids. The parents helped push the kids through the turnstile. They walked away into the parking lot.

My turn.

Good-bye, HorrorLand. Good-bye, Jonathan Chiller.

I grabbed the turnstile. Pushed it.

And let out a scream of pain and horror as a powerful blast shook my body.

It sent me staggering.

Pain jolted every part of me. I dropped to the ground.

Breathe . . . Breathe . . . Come on, breathe, Ray.

I couldn't move.

11

My arms and legs buzzed and shook. I sucked in a deep breath of cool air. I lifted my head slowly. I tried to blink away the yellow and red splotches that flashed in front of my eyes.

The other kids huddled around me. Sam helped pull me to my feet. "You got a *way* powerful shock," he said.

"We could see the flash of electricity," Marco said.

I blinked some more. The pulsing colors were fading away. I took another deep breath. Started to feel normal again.

I turned to the gate. I saw two women walk out without any trouble.

"How did Chiller do that to you?" Andy asked.

"I think I know how," I said. I pulled the Chef Belcher Helper card from my jeans pocket. "Chiller must have planted some kind of sensor in these cards. When the card goes up to the turnstile, it sets off the electrical charge."

"Bet you're right," Marco said. He pulled out his card and studied it. "There's got to be a chip in here that sets off the shock."

"Okay. So let's just throw away our cards and walk out of here," Jessica said.

I liked her. She was bold. She didn't seem to be afraid of anything.

"What did you choose at Chiller's shop the first time you were here?" I asked.

"I told you. A two-headed coin," she replied. "It took my friend and me back to a medieval kingdom. Really. Don't ask me about it. I know you won't believe me."

"I believe you," Marco said. "Chiller can do a lot of weird things. But who says we can't just dump the cards and walk out of here?"

I handed him mine. He collected all the others.

I didn't see any trash cans. We spotted an empty food cart across from the exit. The sign on the side read: CHOCOLATE CHIP SUSHI ICE CREAM. There was no one near it.

Marco pulled open a drawer in the front of the cart and shoved the trading cards inside. He slammed the drawer shut and hurried back to us.

"What are we waiting for?" he cried. "Let's go. We're *outta* here." We all began to walk quickly.

The park had emptied out. I didn't see anyone else around. I started to jog. "I'll go first," I said. "I'll see if it's safe."

I took a deep breath. I grabbed the turnstile.

I clenched all of my muscles. Was I going to get another painful jolt of electricity?

No.

Holding my breath, I started to push the turnstile . . .

. . . and the heavy metal gate came crashing down in front of it. The gate made a clanging roar as it thundered to the pavement.

Trapped. Trapped inside.

I ducked back and glanced up and down the exit. The iron gate had come down like a wall. No way out.

"I . . . don't believe it," Sam said, shaking his head. "We were so close."

"Chiller wins this round," I said.

"Let's get those cards back and find our Helpers," Jessica said. "The faster we find them, the faster we get out of this crazy place."

I spun around. I started to race to the ice cream cart.

I skidded to a stop — and uttered a shocked cry. "Oh, no. I don't *believe* it!"

The cart was gone.

12

Marco grabbed my shoulder. He pointed. "There it goes!"

A fat green-and-purple Horror in a white apron was pushing the cart away.

"Get him!" I cried.

The Horror looked stunned as we ran after him and circled the cart. He stared at us. "You dudes like sushi-frutti ice cream?"

"We need something in your cart," I said. I didn't wait for him to move. I reached over and slid open the top drawer. I grabbed the cards and shut the drawer for him.

"Try a scoop," the Horror said. "I've got lima bean sherbet, too." He made a pouty face when he saw we weren't interested. "Afraid it will spoil your appetites?" he asked.

"Our appetites are already spoiled," Jessica said.

We hurried away. Back to the side of the

Stagger Inn. I passed out the cards. I gave everyone the card they had before.

"We'd better split up," I said.

Andy bit his bottom lip. I could see him thinking hard. "I . . . I don't really want to go on this scavenger hunt alone," he murmured. "Look. I'm not afraid to admit it. I'm scared."

"He's right," Meg said, moving closer to him. "Maybe Chiller wants to split us up. Maybe we stand a better chance if we stick together."

"If we stick together, it just makes it easier for the Hunters," Jessica said.

"What if we go in pairs?" I suggested.

"That might work," Andy said.

"Okay. Let's go in twos," I said. "We'll search for the Helpers. Maybe some of us will get lucky and go home. If anyone is left or in trouble or something, meet behind Chiller's shop in two hours."

"Sounds like a plan," Jessica said.

So we split up into twos. Marco and Jessica. Andy and Meg. That left Sam and me.

Sam squinted at my Helper card. "Hey, I remember that guy," he said. "Chef Belcher. Yeah. I remember his restaurant. Sick. The food was totally sick."

"Do you remember where the restaurant is?" I asked.

Sam nodded. "Follow me."

* * *

We made our way through the empty park. The little sliver of a moon was high overhead now. The air turned cooler. It was too quiet. I wished there were other people around.

I thought about my parents and my brother back home. I wondered if they had discovered I was gone. I wondered if they were in a total panic.

I felt major panic myself. As we followed the path toward Wolfsbane Forest, I kept my eye out for someone carrying a crossbow.

Sam led the way to a tiny place called The Spear-It Café. The sign by the door read: IF YOU CAN SPEAR IT, YOU CAN EAT IT!

We walked in together. It was just a lunch counter with a row of red stools. The air smelled stale and greasy.

On the other side of the counter, I saw a man in a white uniform with a white chef's hat on his head. He stood with his back to us and scraped a fry griddle with a long-handled spatula.

Sam and I took seats at the counter. "Hi," I said. "Are you Chef Belcher?"

He turned around. He pulled off his chef's hat and mopped his sweaty forehead with it. He was bald and red-faced and dripping with sweat. His blue eyes rolled around in his head as if they were loose or something.

"Aah, welcome, victims!" he cried, rubbing his hands together.

I guess he was trying to be funny.

Before we could say anything, he whipped his hand up — and trapped a fly inside it. "Got to be fast," he said.

He carried the fly to a big pot on the stove and dropped it in. "It's my famous Everything Stew," he said. "Flies give it flavor." He winked at us. "Just because I went to barber school doesn't mean I don't know the right ingredients to use."

I swallowed. My stomach felt fluttery. "We were told to talk to you," I said.

"Sure," Belcher replied. "First, try the stew." He scooped two big helpings into bowls and carried them to the counter. "Go ahead. It's on the house."

Sam and I gazed into our bowls. The stew was crawling with flies.

"Sam and I aren't very hungry," I said.

Belcher wiped more sweat off with his chef's hat. Then he pulled the hat back on his head.

I held up the Helper card. He took it and studied it. His wild eyes rolled around crazily.

"Not a bad picture of me," he murmured. "Do you know which is my best side?"

"Which side?" I asked.

"The *out*side!" He chuckled. He slid the card around in his greasy fingers.

"We're playing a game," Sam said. "We're supposed to find six red chests."

"My chest is red," Belcher said. "I have a pretty bad rash."

I think he was making another joke. But Sam and I didn't laugh.

This guy was totally annoying.

"You're a Helper, right?" I said. "Can you help us find one of the little red chests?"

"Maybe," he said. He scratched his chin. "I can't get it for you. That's against the rules. But I can lead you in the right direction."

"Awesome," I said.

Belcher scrunched up his chef's hat and dropped it onto the counter. He pulled off the stained apron and let it fall to the floor. "Follow me," he said.

He led us out of the restaurant, around the side to the back. Clouds covered the moon. There were no lights back here.

We followed a narrow dirt path through the trees. The park was silent. All I could hear was my own heartbeat and the rustling whispers of the trees overhead.

Belcher took long strides and didn't look back. Sam trotted up to me. It was so dark, I could barely see him. "Where is he taking us?"

I shrugged. "We have to trust him. He's a Helper."

The narrow path curved through tall trees. Sometimes Belcher disappeared into the shadows.

I heard a shrill animal howl. It made the skin on the back of my neck prickle. The howl was joined by other howls.

Wolf howls? They almost sounded human.

The path ended suddenly at a tall wire fence. Clouds slid away from the moon. Pale light poured down over a sign halfway up the fence: WOLFSBANE FOREST.

13

"I was here before," Sam said. His voice came out in a whisper. "I'm totally into animals. My first time in HorrorLand, I went straight to the Werewolf Petting Zoo. It was great. But this forest is way creepy at night."

We followed Belcher to a gate. "Padlocked," he said. "The forest closes at dusk. Too dangerous after dark."

Was he *trying* to scare us? If so, he was doing an excellent job. The prickly feeling at the back of my neck spread over my whole body. I realized I was breathing hard.

"Know the difference between me and the werewolves?" Belcher asked. "The werewolves like their meat *uncooked*! Hahaha."

This guy was about as funny as a bee sting on your butt.

"Are we going in here?" I asked. "Is there a treasure chest hidden in here?"

He didn't answer my question. "Follow me," he said. He motioned us forward.

We walked along the high fence. Tall grass slapped at my jeans. I stared through the metal wires. I could see only darkness on the other side.

Another howl — very nearby — made me jump.

"The forest is closed, but I know how to get in," Belcher said. In the moonlight, I saw that his face and forehead were drenched with sweat.

He grabbed a section of the wire fence with both hands and tugged. The fence didn't move. He pulled again.

This time a narrow section began to slide over the tall grass. He pried it open, a space just wide enough for the three of us to squeeze through.

I took a few steps, then stopped. A long, mournful howl sounded just up ahead.

"Is it — a real wolf?" I stammered.

Belcher shook his head. "No. A real *werewolf.*"

"I mean, really," I said.

"Really," Belcher insisted. "Don't you believe in werewolves?"

"I . . . don't . . . think so," I said.

"How about the tooth fairy?" he said. He started to laugh, but another wolf howl cut him off.

"Where is the red chest?" I asked. "Is it near here?" I shuddered. "Can we find it and get out of here?"

Belcher mopped his forehead with his shirt-sleeve. "This way," he said.

He started walking over the tall grass, deeper into the forest. He disappeared in the darkness. I could hear his footsteps up ahead.

Sam and I cried out as piercing howls rang in our ears.

I pictured hungry wolf creatures hiding behind the fat tree trunks, preparing to leap out and attack. I could see the drool pouring over their jagged fangs as they opened their jaws to rip apart our flesh.

Yes, I've seen too many horror movies. I like scary movies and books. I like creepy things.

But not when they are actually *happening* to me.

The trees covered us. So thick I couldn't see the night sky. The grass gave way to patchy dirt. Dead leaves crackled under my shoes.

"Ouch!" I let out a cry as I stumbled over a fallen tree branch. Pain shot through my leg.

"Chef Belcher," I said, "are you sure there's a chest hidden here?"

He didn't answer.

"Chef Belcher?" I called.

I listened for his footsteps.

Silence.

"Hey, what's up?" Sam called. "Where are you?"

I cupped my hands around my mouth. "Chef Belcher?"

No reply.

A chill slid down my back. I spun all around, searching for him.

He had vanished.

14

"Hey — he's supposed to be our Helper," Sam said. "What a jerk."

I took a deep breath. "Belcher said he couldn't get the chest for us," I said. "He said he could only lead the way."

"Look around, Ray. We're out in the middle of nowhere," Sam said. "I don't even know which way to walk back. He didn't help us — he got us lost."

"But this is the kind of creepy place where Chiller would hide a chest," I argued.

A long, low wolf howl made both of us freeze.

"We have to get out of here," Sam said. He pulled my sleeve. "Come on. I've studied wolves. I told you, I'm an animal nut. But that doesn't sound like a normal wolf howl to me."

I started to follow Sam — but I stopped. And pointed. "Whoa. What's that?"

Straight ahead of us, the trees opened. Pale moonlight washed down on a small round clearing.

And in the middle of the clearing, I could see a low black mound, like a tree stump or a tiny hill.

Squinting hard, I saw a small rectangular box resting on top of the hill.

I slapped Sam on the shoulder. "See it? Belcher led us here. That's the treasure chest."

"Yessss!" We slapped each other a high five. Then, without another word, we went running into the clearing.

In the moonlight, the dark mound appeared to glow. And move.

Still too dark to see it clearly. It was nearly as tall as Sam and me. And that was definitely a small box sitting on top of it.

"Whoa. What's that sound?" Sam pulled me back.

We both stopped, breathing hard. I heard a buzzing, low and muffled.

Was it coming from the low hill? Yes.

Walking side by side, we crept up close. The buzz became a steady, droning roar. And when we were close enough to see clearly, I let out a gasp.

"What are those?" I asked Sam in a hushed whisper.

The hill was *alive*. It wasn't dirt or a rock. It was a living, pulsing, buzzing thing.

"Wasps!" Sam cried. "Ray — look out. Millions of them. Millions of wasps."

Yes. We were staring at some kind of enormous wasps' nest.

Wings buzzing, the wasps bounced off each other, clumped together, darting in and out. An enormous, deadly mountain of wasps.

And at the top — I could see it clearly now — a small treasure chest.

Sam stumbled back. He swatted a wasp off his face.

I realized I was standing too close to the nest. My head began to itch. I swiped two or three wasps from my face. My skin tingled all up and down my body. I danced and twitched and waved my arms.

I staggered back. Wasps clung to my shirt-sleeves. I swung my hands hard and sent them flying back to the nest.

The buzzing rang in my head, surrounded me.

Sam swatted wasps off the front of his T-shirt. He plucked one off the back of my neck. The wasp was gone, but my skin still tingled.

Wasps darted back and forth in front of my eyes. I felt a prickle on my forehead and slapped a wasp away.

"We're *outta* here!" Sam declared. He spun away and started to run back to the trees.

"No — wait," I called after him. "The chest. I've got to get that chest."

I turned back and stared at it. Wasps hovered over the chest, buzzing, lighting on it, then flitting off. Hundreds of gleaming wasps slid down the nest, like lava down a mountain.

"You can't grab the chest," Sam said. "You need gloves, Ray. You'll get a million stings."

"I have to try," I said. "We can't come this close and not get the chest."

I swiped a wasp off my forehead.

My fast move startled a bunch of them. Buzzing louder, they leaped off the nest. They hovered for a few seconds, then settled back down.

"If we had a shovel or something, we could make them all scatter," Sam said. "You know. Sweep them away. Then you could just grab the chest and run."

"But we don't have a shovel," I said. "We don't have anything. I — I just have to be *fast*."

A gust of wind made the wasps buzz louder. They rose up, then settled back. They swarmed over each other, crawling over each other, darting in and out.

"Ray — don't." Sam grabbed my arm.

But I pulled free and stepped up to the pulsing, buzzing mountain of wasps.

I took a deep breath. Stared hard at the little red chest, half buried in buzzing wasp bodies. Shut my eyes for a second. Opened them.

I stuck my hand into the gleaming, swirling nest — and grabbed the chest.

"OOWWWWWWWWWW!"

15

The loud cry of pain came from behind me.

"Sam?"

I swung the chest away from the wasps' nest. Gripping it tightly, I stumbled toward him. "What's wrong? What happened?"

Sam rubbed the back of his neck. "Sorry I screamed. I got stung." He pulled the stinger from his skin. Then he rubbed his neck some more.

"Look!" I cried breathlessly. I held the chest up in front of me. "Got it."

"Excellent!" Sam cried. He pumped his fists in the air. "Belcher led us in the right direction," he said. "He's a creep. But he was a good Helper."

He gazed around, shivering. "Wish he was here to lead us back."

"We'll find our way back," I said. "Then we'll find *your* Helper. Who is it?"

"Mondo the Magical."

"We'll find him and find your red chest," I said. "Come on — let's roll."

Sam stared at the chest in my hand. "Aren't you going to open it? Ray, go ahead. Check it out."

"Oh. Yeah. Okay." Behind me, the buzzing from the giant wasps' nest grew till it became a dull roar. Carrying the chest in front of me, I took several steps toward the trees.

I stopped at the edge of the clearing and turned to Sam. "Here goes."

I pulled the lid open.

BOINNNNNG.

I *screamed* as a grinning clown popped out.

My heart pounded from the surprise. The chest fell out of my hands.

I bent down and picked it up. The plastic clown bobbed on a spring. It held a tiny sign on its striped chest:

YOU LOSE.

"A stupid joke," I said to Sam. I tossed the chest to him. "A stupid jack-in-the-box."

Sam's mouth dropped open. "This is horrible! We — we're never getting out of here! He — he tricked us!" He handed the box back to me.

"No. Come on. It's a game — remember?" I said. "This is part of Chiller's game. We have to keep searching. Find the chest with the Horror in it."

Sam shook his head. "Hope you're right."

"Let's go," I said. I tossed the chest into the dirt and started to run.

But I didn't get far and neither did Sam.

We were surrounded by wolves.

No. Not wolves.

Wolf *creatures* staggering toward us on two legs.

They had wolf faces, snouts open as they growled and grunted, snapping their jagged teeth. Furry wolf bodies but human-shaped arms and human legs. Their big feet were also covered in fur, but I saw human toes on the ends. Their tails stood straight behind them, stiff and alert.

"Those aren't real animals. They have to be actors," Sam murmured. He called to them. "Awesome costumes!"

I wasn't so sure they were costumes. My legs were trembling. I had a bad feeling in the pit of my stomach.

"Listen, we're playing a game here," Sam told them. "And we kind of got lost. Can you tell us how to get out?"

Snarling, the wolf creatures formed a tight circle around us. Two of them tossed back their heads and let out howls.

As they circled, the wolf creatures lowered their heads. Their eyes glowed red like animal eyes. They circled faster. I counted eight of them.

"Come on, guys," Sam said. "We're sorry. We know we're not supposed to be here this late. But can you give us a break?"

They all began to snarl at once. They lowered their bodies until they stood on all fours. They arched their backs. They growled ferociously like attack dogs.

"Sam — they — they're NOT human!" I screamed.

Before we could move, they leaped at us, roaring, gnashing their massive teeth, huge taloned paws raised to attack.

I opened my mouth to scream, but no sound came out.

I raised my hands in front of me to shield myself. And gasped in surprise when I heard a loud *THWOCCCK*.

I followed the sound — and saw a long arrow trembling in the trunk of a tree inches from my head.

The wolf creatures stopped — almost in midair — and backed off.

THWOCCCK.

Another arrow whistled just above my head. It sailed past the same tree trunk.

Whimpering, the wolf creatures retreated.

Sam and I didn't move. Another arrow split the air. This one shot right past my head and sailed past the tree.

And then I heard a voice from somewhere in the trees. Chef Belcher!

"Look out, boys!" he shouted. "Someone is firing at you. There's a Hunter here!"

The wolf creatures let out frightened cries — and took off. Some ran on two legs. Others dropped to the ground and scrambled away on all fours.

Sam and I didn't have time to celebrate their retreat. Another arrow split the air between us.

We dived away from it.

"Get going, guys!" Chef Belcher shouted. "This Hunter means business! *MOVE!*"

We took off, running toward Belcher's voice. We rocketed through the clearing and back into the trees. No sign of Belcher.

"Chef Belcher? Where are you?" I screamed. "Chef Belcher?"

Silence.

We ran until we couldn't run anymore. Then we huddled behind some bushes and tried to catch our breath.

"Am I enjoying this game?" Sam cried. "I don't *think* so."

I sighed. "What if — what if *all* the chests are jokes?"

Sam's dark eyes widened in fear. "We have to tell the others," he said.

17

The forest was silent now. Sam and I wandered through the trees till we found the tall wire fence. We slipped back out and made our way to the path that led to the front of the park.

HorrorLand was totally closed. The lights had been dimmed. The shops and restaurants were empty. The food carts had been abandoned. I didn't see any Horrors or guards.

We walked past The Play Pen, the carnival games area. A big sign read: IT'S NOT HOW MUCH YOU WIN OR LOSE BUT HOW MUCH YOU SCREAM YOUR HEAD OFF! Helium balloons on strings bobbed and flapped in the evening breeze.

A skinny orange cat slithered past our feet. I jumped back to keep from tripping over it. The cat turned. It had only one eye.

"Even the cats are scary here," I murmured.

"Where are we going?" Sam asked. "Are we just wandering around, trying to find the others?"

"No," I said. "I know where to go. That serious-looking kid with the real dark eyes? The dude who's into comic books? Marco? I saw his Helper card. It was Murder the Clown."

"Cute. So where does Murder the Clown hang out?"

"The Haunted Theater," I said. "They do a ghost clown show there."

We trotted across the empty Zombie Plaza. Some of the shops were still lighted, but I didn't see any people or Horrors. Carried by the wind, a paper cup bounced along the ground as if walking with us.

The Haunted Theater was easy to find. It looked like a big castle, with turrets poking up on both sides. The sign above the ticket window read: MONDO THE MAGICAL. AND GHOST CLOWN REVUE. CAN YOU DIE LAUGHING?

There was no one in the ticket booth. I tried one of the front doors to the theater. Locked.

"Marco and that real tall girl, Jessica, went together," I told Sam. "Maybe they're inside, looking for the clown."

Sam tried another door. Also locked. "Let's go around the back," he said.

We walked around the side of the building, keeping close to the tall stone wall. Near the back, I saw someone leaning against a narrow door.

As we walked closer, I saw that he was a clown. The saddest-looking clown I've ever seen.

His painted mouth drooped down as if he was bawling. His sad eyes were rimmed with black, and painted teardrops fell down his white cheeks. Even his straw-blond hair drooped down the sides of his face.

He was dressed in rags. His red clown ruffle was torn and stained. The buttons on his striped shirt were all missing. The shirt hung open, revealing a ripped undershirt. His baggy, wrinkled pants had holes in the knees. The tops of his big brown shoes were loose from their soles.

He didn't seem to see us until we were standing right in front of him. Then he slowly raised his head. "Sorry. No autographs," he said. His voice was harsh, gravelly.

"We — we're looking for someone," I said.

He squinted at me. "So?"

"Can you help us?" Sam asked.

The clown turned to Sam and frowned even harder. "Help you? Do I look like your *mother*?"

This guy had to be the *least* funny clown I'd ever seen.

He scratched his chest through the torn undershirt. "Who are you looking for?"

"Murder the Clown," I said. "I think our two friends —"

"You have two friends?" the clown interrupted. "Big *whoop*."

"Do you know where we can find Murder?" I said.

He nodded. His droopy hair fell over his face. "He's in the basement. I killed him. HAHAHAHAHA."

Did he really expect us to laugh at that?

He pulled open the door. It squeaked as it slid open. "Go ahead," the clown rasped. "Murder is rehearsing downstairs. Go. Have a picnic. HAHAHAHA."

His laughing sounded more like crying. Whatever made this guy decide to be a clown?

Sam and I slipped past him. I blinked several times, waiting for my eyes to adjust to the dim light. We seemed to be in a huge, empty room. A storage room, maybe.

I jumped as the clown slammed the door shut behind us. Were we locked in?

Sam and I gazed around. I heard water dripping somewhere. Faint music from far away. A fat gray rat scampered along the back wall. Its tail swung behind it on the floor.

"He said Murder is in the basement." My voice echoed in the big, empty room. Our shoes thudded loudly on the concrete floor as we made our way toward a doorway across from us.

Sam shivered. "I don't like this place. It's creeping me out."

"Let's just find Marco and Jessica," I said. "Maybe they're having better luck than we did."

We walked through a long, straight hallway. It felt like a tunnel, narrow, with low ceilings. I could hear voices at the other end. But when we stepped out into a circle of rooms, the voices stopped.

Sam and I walked around the circle, peeking into rooms. They were dressing rooms. Mirrors and makeup tables and folding chairs.

A winding metal staircase stood between two dressing rooms. Our shoes clanged as we followed it down to another circle of rooms.

"This must be the basement," I said. "But I don't see any rehearsal rooms."

Sam led the way into another tunnel-like hallway. The air grew cooler. We followed the tunnel to another big, empty room.

"Hey!" I cried out as something brushed my face.

Spiderwebs?

No. I didn't see any.

Sam shook his head hard. He waved his hand as if brushing away a fly.

"What was that? Did you feel something?" I asked.

Something cold brushed the back of my neck. It felt like icy fingers.

I spun around. No one there.

Sam kept trying to brush something away. "Something is touching my face!" he cried. "Something cold."

I felt a rush of frigid air through my hair. And then icy fingers squeezed my ears.

"Hey!" I let out a frightened shout.

I spun all around. I bumped into Sam and nearly knocked him over. I could still feel the cold touch of something invisible.

"Do you — do you think this theater really is *haunted*?" My voice cracked on the word.

Sam shook his head again. "I don't believe in ghosts," he said. "But . . . something was touching my face. YAAAII!"

He jumped and dodged away.

"What's wrong?" I cried.

"Ray, I felt someone squeeze my neck!" Sam cried. "Ohh, it's cold. So cold." He rubbed his neck. His eyes were wide with fear.

"Let's get out of here," I said. "Which way do we go?"

"I don't know," Sam replied. "I'm all turned around."

I pointed. Another stairway led down.

"But we're already in the basement," Sam said.

"Guess there are two basements," I said. I stepped to the top of the stairway and listened. Silence down there. And total darkness.

"This was a bad idea," Sam said. "We're all alone in this huge theater, and we're totally lost."

"Let's try that door," I said. We crossed the big room. The door was closed. I reached for the doorknob.

But the door swung open before I could grab it. And a fat, ugly clown — with a hatchet buried in his skull — leaped in front of us.

Murder!

"WHOA!" Sam and I both shouted in surprise.

Murder tossed back his head and cackled. "CAUGHT you!" he cried. He cackled some more, an ugly, crazy laugh. "Are you two afraid of clowns?"

He didn't give us a chance to answer.

"You SHOULD be!" he said. "It's SHOWtime!"

18

Sam and I stood gaping at the big clown. His eyes were big and black. His eyebrows were shaped like upside-down V's. It made him look totally evil. His huge red-painted mouth was locked in an ugly grin.

The ax blade was buried halfway into his bald head. The handle stuck out at an angle behind him.

Jessica and Marco came walking into the room. They both seemed very surprised to see Sam and me.

"Know how I got this hatchet buried in my head?" Murder demanded.

"No," Sam and I said together.

"*Neither do I!*" he screamed. "Hahahaha. That joke KILLS the audience! I murder them! I *murder* them!"

Marco and Jessica rushed up to Sam and me. "We have been trying to talk to him," Marco said. "But we can't get a word in."

"What are you guys doing here?" Jessica asked.

"Our Helper led us to a red chest," I said. "But it was a joke. A stupid jack-in-the-box. No Horror inside."

"Chiller may not be playing fair," Sam told them. "And a Hunter started firing at us. The hunting game has started."

"You think Chiller hid a bunch of joke chests all over?" Jessica asked. "Just to keep us busy while the Hunters *hunt* us?"

I shrugged. "I hope not. We have to keep searching. It's our only hope of getting out of here."

Murder acted as if he hadn't heard us. "You know what's *really* funny?" he demanded. "I'll give you a hint. It rests on your neck! Maybe it's your *face*? HAHAHA."

"Hurry. Show him your card," I told Marco. "Maybe he'll help us find a real chest."

"You want card tricks?" Murder said. He pulled out a deck of cards and shoved it in front of my face. "Pick a card. Go ahead, kiddo. Pick a card."

I didn't want to stand there doing card tricks. I was desperate to find out if there were chests with Horrors in them so we could get home. But what choice did I have? I pulled a card out of the deck. A three of clubs.

"Okay, tear it in half," Murder said. "Go ahead. Tear it."

I tore the card in half.

"Now tear the halves in half," Murder instructed. I did it. "Now tear them in half again. Go ahead. Tear them into tiny little pieces."

I did it.

"Okay," Murder said, "hold the pieces over your head. Now let them fall. HAPPY NEW YEAR! Hahahaha! That joke KILLS. It kills!"

"Very funny," I said. "But don't you wonder why we're here so late at night? We're on a scavenger hunt. And we're in a real hurry."

Marco shoved the trading card at Murder. "You're our Helper, right? You're supposed to help us?"

The clown took the card into his white-gloved hand. He studied it for a moment. "Who is this handsome dude?"

"Can you help us?" I asked.

"Yeah, I can help you," he said. "Follow me. All of you. The more the *scarier*!"

"You can help us find a treasure chest with a Horror inside it?" Jessica asked.

He nodded. "Sure I can. You can trust a man with an ax buried in his head — right?"

No one replied. What can you say to that?

Murder led the way upstairs and out the side door of the theater. We followed him through the plaza and along one of the dimly lit, twisting paths through the park.

We passed a sign that read: WELCOME TO THE BLACK LAGOON. In the distance, I could see a lake. The water shimmered under the pale moonlight.

"This is where they have the Bottomless Canoe Rides," Murder said. "Lots of fun — unless you hate swimming for your life."

In the lagoon, low waves splashed gently against the shore. Murder led us along a picket fence. On the other side of the fence, I saw a narrow, flat beach. The sand looked blue under the moonlight.

We stopped at a gate. "This beach is closed," Murder announced. "But I can let you in. There's a treasure chest half buried in the middle of the beach."

He fiddled with the lock on the gate, and it sprung open. He pushed the gate.

"Go ahead." He waved us in. "Find the chest. One of you will be able to go home. It has a Horror inside it. Trust me. Clowns never lie."

Was that a joke?

It didn't matter. We stepped past him onto the sand. It was soft and dry. My shoes sank into it as I followed Marco and Jessica.

"Good luck," Murder called after us. I heard the gate close behind us.

"Maybe it will be easier to walk if we take our shoes off," Jessica said. "This sand is so soft."

"Let's just find the chest," I said. And then I saw it. Halfway down the beach. A dark rectangle poking up from the sand.

The four of us began running toward it. But we didn't get far.

My shoes sank deep into the sand. Over my ankles. Then even deeper.

"The sand is wet here," I said. "I'm kind of sinking."

I tried to pull my feet back up to the top. But I couldn't budge them. To my shock, I sank even farther. The sand was up to my knees.

I turned and saw the other kids struggling.

"I'm sinking," Marco said. "Sinking fast." He sounded more surprised than frightened.

But then I saw something that made me shudder. A sign half hidden in shadow on the picket fence. It read: QUICKSAND BEACH. DROP IN ANYTIME.

"Hey — it's quicksand!" I shouted. My voice came out high and shrill. "That clown — he didn't tell us this was quicksand!"

I struggled to pull my feet out of the wet muck. But they were stuck. I squirmed and tried to twist myself out.

But my straining and struggling only made me sink faster. The sand was up to my waist now. The cold and wet seeped through my jeans.

How deep is it?

"Hey — help!" Marco cried a few feet ahead of

me. He was twisting his body. Slapping his hands on the sand.

Jessica was trying to scoop the sand away from her with both hands. But the more she moved, the deeper she sank.

I swung my body around to face the gate. "Help us!" I shouted. "Hey — Murder! Help us! Get us out of here."

"You're supposed to be a Helper," Jessica cried. "So — help us!"

"He — he's gone," Sam stuttered.

Sam was right. There was no one at the gate. No one in sight.

The cold, wet sand slid up over my waist. I couldn't move my legs. I grabbed the surface of the sand and tried to hoist myself up. But I wasn't strong enough.

The sand crept higher quickly. In a few seconds . . . in a few seconds . . . I could be buried. Totally buried under the sand.

I turned and saw the others. Jessica was buried to her waist. Her hair was touching the surface of the sand behind her. She was twisting and squirming. But it only made her sink deeper.

Beside me, Sam struggled silently. Trying to twist his body free. But he was sinking fast, too.

Marco's hands pushed against the sand. He grunted and groaned, straining to free himself.

The sand make a sick *gluppppp* sound as it pulled him down. It was almost up to his armpits. He opened his mouth in a terrified, hoarse cry.

I gritted my teeth. I strained every muscle.

But no way could I free myself. No way could I stop my body from sinking deeper.

"Hey!" I shrieked. "Help! Please! Is anyone there? Can anyone hear me? Help us! Anyone?"

19

No reply.

No one there to hear our screams.

The smell of the sand invaded my nose. I could almost taste it. Feel it in my mouth, so grainy and dry. Filling my mouth. Choking my throat. Choking me . . .

No.

My feet touched something. Something hard.

"Hey!" I stopped sinking.

Jessica started to scream — but stopped. Silence over the beach. The others had hit bottom, too.

"I — I really thought we were going to go under," Jessica said, her voice trembling.

"The HorrorLand people just want to scare us," I said. "They don't want to *kill* us."

The treasure chest sat only a few feet in front of us.

I leaned forward and pushed hard. Pushed some sand away.

I leaned into it. More quicksand moved. I'd made a small space in front of me.

I pushed harder. Then I slapped my hands onto the sand. Using all my strength, I pulled myself to the top.

Then I lay gasping for breath, sprawled on my stomach on the surface of the sand.

When I raised my head, I saw that Sam had also pulled himself out. He was crawling carefully toward Jessica. He grabbed her arms and slowly lifted her from the wet quicksand. She sat on her knees, catching her breath.

Marco was the last to free himself. He sat carefully and brushed the wet clumps of sand off his clothes. "Yuck. This is worse than The Ooze," he said.

"How can you think about comic books when we're in the middle of a quicksand pit?" Jessica said. "Let's get that chest and get out of here."

We didn't say another word. We all crawled carefully over the sand.

My knees kept sinking into the sand. I could feel a force pulling me, pulling me down. But I moved quickly, forcing myself forward.

Jessica reached the chest first. She grabbed it in both hands and lifted it from the sand. "Who wants to go home first?" she cried.

"It's Marco's," I said. "It was his Helper card, his Helper who brought us here. This has to be Marco's turn."

Jessica handed the chest to Marco.

He held it in front of him, gazing at it. He brushed sand off the bottom. "I'm almost afraid to open it," he said.

"Go ahead. Don't keep us in suspense," Jessica said. She gave Marco's shoulder a gentle push. "Open it."

We moved closer. My heart was racing. My eyes were locked on the little red box. Would a clown pop out?

Marco gripped the lid and pulled it open.

He reached inside and pulled out something white. He held it up. A Horror. A three-inch-tall white Horror.

It had tiny eyes and short horns that curled from the top of its head. Its face and body and uniform were solid white.

"Yes! Yes!" Marco held it in one hand and pumped his other fist in the air in triumph. "We found one." He turned to us. "Are you really going to let me go home?"

We all quickly agreed. "It's yours, Marco. Your turn."

He thanked us. "Good luck, guys," he said. "Go find your Horrors and get out of here."

He wrapped his hands around the little white Horror. "It's been real, guys," he said. "Catch you later."

He closed his eyes and held the Horror in front of his chest.

We watched in silence. The word *go go go* repeated in my mind. I held my breath and waited for Marco to disappear.

He squeezed the little Horror in both hands. Squeezed it tight. Tighter.

Then his eyes opened wide. "Oh, wow. I don't *believe* it!" he moaned.

Marco held up the Horror. It had crumbled into pieces.

"It's chocolate," he said. "White chocolate."

We gaped at him. Jessica's mouth fell open. She pressed her hands to the sides of her face. "It's . . . not a real Horror?"

"Yeah. Some kind of joke," Marco grumbled. He heaved the Horror pieces onto the sand.

I took the chest and peered inside. On the bottom, I saw a white card with two words printed in black:

YOU LOSE.

"So far, we found two chests," I said. "Two chests and no Horrors."

From the other side of the fence, I heard loud laughter. I recognized it. Murder the Clown.

"Sorry about that, dudes!" he shouted. "That's the problem when you play games with Jonathan Chiller! He CHEATS!"

I couldn't see him. I could only hear him. "Murder — help us out of here," I called.

"Yeah. Open the gate!" Sam shouted. "Let us out."

"You forgot to say pretty please!" Murder shouted. "You should always mind your manners when you're sitting on quicksand! Hahahaha!"

"Please hurry!" Marco cried.

"Are you going to take us to a *real* treasure chest?" Jessica shouted.

"I'm a Helper — aren't I?" he yelled back. "What do I look like — a *clown*?"

I heard a shrill whistling sound. I felt a rush of air as an arrow flew inches from my head.

Jessica and Marco screamed. They fell flat onto their stomachs. They struggled to stay on top of the quicksand.

Another arrow narrowly missed me. It made a *thwoccck* sound as it landed in the quicksand.

"A Hunter!" Murder the Clown cried. "Hurry! Get to the gate, everyone!"

I started to move across the sand. But stopped with a gasp as another arrow whistled toward us. It missed my leg by an inch or two and crashed into the wet ground.

"Hurry! You're sitting ducks in there!" Murder shouted from the other side of the fence. "Get out! Get away from the Hunter!"

I reached forward and pulled the arrow from the sand. Raising it close, I let out a startled cry.

No suction cup at the end.

Instead, I was staring at a metal point. I pressed my finger against it. The arrowhead was deadly sharp.

"They — they're using *real* arrows!" I screamed to the others. "This isn't a game. They're really hunting us!"

We scrambled across the quicksand, kicking sand in front of us, struggling to the gate. I reached it first and burst onto solid ground. I had the arrow still gripped tightly in my fist.

"Look!" I cried to Murder. "Look!" I waved the arrow in his face.

"Looks like an arrow," Murder said. "Chiller didn't tell us. He —"

"Hey!" I cried. My eyes lowered to the crossbow on the ground by the fence. The four of us ran over to it.

"The Hunter dropped it and ran," the clown said. "You're not hurt, right?"

"But what did he look like?" Jessica demanded. "The Hunter — what did he look like?"

"I didn't get a good look at him," Murder said. "I can't describe him. He was dressed in black. He shot at you and then he ran."

"We've got to warn the other two kids," I said. "What were their names?"

"Meg and Andy," Jessica said. "Meg had a Helper card with a fortune-teller on it."

"Madame Doom," Murder said. "Go. Tell them."

The four of us took off, running to the plaza.

"We have to warn Meg and Andy the arrows are real," I said.

"And the little chests don't have Horrors in them," Sam said. "What are we going to do?"

Running beside me, Jessica let out a sigh. "If there are no hidden Horrors, how do we get home?"

A chill tightened the back of my neck. "Is that the point of Chiller's twisted game?" I said. "He's going to hunt us down — and we're NEVER going home!"

21

We found Meg and Andy in a corner of Zombie Plaza. They were standing in front of Madame Doom's glass fortune-teller booth.

The booth looked like the ticket window at a movie theater. Behind the glass, I saw the wooden fortune-teller. She had black hair, a red-and-purple turban wrapped around her head, loads of beads around her neck, a bright red dress.

Her painted face had dark, staring eyes, red cheeks, and a red-lipsticked mouth turned down in a cold frown. A neon sign above the booth read: MADAME DOOM KNOWS EVERYTHING AND MORE.

Meg and Andy spun away from the booth as we came running up to them. Meg held up her Helper card. "Andy and I searched all around here. But we haven't seen any little chest."

"Why are you guys here?" Andy asked. "You couldn't find any chests?"

"We found two chests," I said breathlessly. "And they were jokes. They didn't have the Horrors in them."

"Chiller lied to us," Sam said. "His whole game is a cheat."

"The Hunters are using real arrows," Jessica said. "We're in big danger."

We all started talking at once. Meg and Andy looked totally confused.

"What do you think we should do?" Andy asked. "Should we stop hunting for the chests and try to find help?"

"I can't believe this is happening," Meg said, her eyes wide with fear. "I played one of Chiller's games. I told you. He brought me here last Halloween. It was a crazy, twisted game. Totally disturbing and frightening. But he played fair. He let me go home when the game was over."

I stared at her. "He isn't playing fair this time."

"We need to find a Helper who will really help us," Jessica said.

"Chef Belcher and Murder the Clown tried to help," Sam said. "But . . . it didn't work out. We were nearly hit by arrows both times."

Meg tapped her hand on the front of the glass booth. "Maybe Madame Doom is a Helper who will help," she said. "Let's see what she says we should do."

"Hurry," I said. My eyes swept the deserted plaza. "Hunters could be coming for us. We can't just stand here."

Meg reached into her jeans pocket and pulled out a coin. She dropped the coin in a slot. The machine inside the booth made a *clugg clugg* sound as it started to move.

We all stared at the wooden mannequin. Nothing happened. Then we heard a creaking sound. Madame Doom's hand dropped down, out of sight.

The machine chugged and creaked. Slowly, Madame Doom's hand raised itself. The hand held a small white card.

Madame Doom began to slide the card toward the small opening in the glass. Slowly, the hand creaked and slid forward.

Meg reached into the booth for the card — and the wooden hand clamped around her hand.

"*Ow!* Let go!" Meg cried.

She pulled hard. But the wooden fingers stayed clamped tightly around her hand.

Meg pulled again. But she couldn't free herself.

The mannequin's eyes seemed to glare at her. The red lips moved. The mouth dropped open.

Meg started to scream. "She won't let go! Help me! She's *squeezing* my hand. *Ow!* It hurts! It really hurts!"

22

I rushed up beside Meg. I slid my hand through the small opening.

"*Ow!* It's tightening!" Meg cried. Her hand was bright red.

I grabbed the wooden fingers. They were hot to the touch. I struggled to pry them back.

But they wouldn't let go of Meg's hand. I tried again. Pulled two fingers back.

And Meg slid her hand free.

"*Ow!* I don't believe it!" she cried. "Is that thing broken? Or was it deliberately set to grab me?" She shook her hand, trying to shake away the pain. It was red and swollen.

"Where's the fortune card?" Andy asked.

I glanced down. The card had fallen to the pavement. I picked it up and handed it to Meg. "Go ahead — read it."

She gripped the card in her good hand. And she read it to us:

"I can help you and your friends. Meet me at my house."

"House?" I said. "Isn't this booth her house?"

Meg shook her head. "No. There's a house. I remember it. I remember the crystal ball. And a woman who looks just like the wooden Madame Doom."

"You mean she's *real*?" Jessica asked.

"Do you remember where her house is?" Sam asked.

Meg thought hard. "I think it's near the Tunnel of Screams." She pointed. "That way."

Meg was right. We found the house easily, across from the Tunnel of Screams. Even though the park was closed, shrill screams continued to blare from the tunnel. Horrified shrieks and screams of men and women, boys and girls, repeating over and over.

"Someone forgot to shut that off," I said.

"Maybe it just goes forever," Sam said with a shiver.

We turned to the house. It looked like a little gingerbread cottage. A purple light in the front window reflected off a crystal ball. Red drapes blocked the view into the house.

A lighted sign above the red front door read: FORTUNES TOLD & LOST. The six of us moved toward the front door. "Think she's in there?" I asked.

"Only one way to find out," Andy said. He grabbed the silver doorknob. "I'll go in first," he said. "If it's a trap, all six of us shouldn't go in there."

"A trap?" Meg exclaimed. "Why would it be a trap? She's supposed to be a Helper."

"I know what I'm doing," Andy said. His dark eyes glared at her. "I'll go in. See if Madame Doom is really here. See if it's safe. Then I'll open the door and call you in."

"We should all go in," I said. "Meg is right. We need her help — fast."

Andy ignored me. He grabbed the doorknob again. "If I don't come back for you in *two minutes* . . . then come in and get me."

"No, wait —"

"Andy, stop —"

But he had his mind made up. The stubborn guy wouldn't listen to us.

Andy pushed open the red door. I could see purple light inside. He disappeared into the little house. The door closed behind him.

We fell silent. We stood in front of the house, gazing at the crystal ball in the window. Listening. Waiting.

My mind whirred. Thought after thought flew past my brain.

We shouldn't just stand out here.

We should go inside and see what's going on.

Why did Andy insist on going in alone?

I stared at the door, thinking hard. Waiting.

"How much time has gone by?" Meg asked in a trembling voice.

Before anyone could answer, we heard a scream from inside the house. A high, shrill scream of pain and horror.

"It — it's *Andy*!" Meg cried.

23

We rushed the door.

I got there first. I turned the knob. Lowered my shoulder. And shoved the door open wide.

I stepped blinking into the purple light. It took a long time to focus my eyes.

I saw a beaded curtain over a back doorway. A table with a purple tablecloth. A crystal ball rested on a small pedestal. A black cat on the mantelpiece. It didn't move. It was stuffed.

Sam and Meg bumped up behind me. Jessica pressed herself against the wall. Marco stood at the front door, his expression tense.

The beaded curtain shook and opened, making a rattling sound. A large woman stepped into the room. Madame Doom.

She looked exactly like the wooden mannequin in the glass booth. A red-and-purple scarf covered most of her black hair. She had the same dark eyes and red cheeks. Her long red skirt brushed the floor as she came toward us.

"Thank goodness you're here," she said in a deep voice. "Do you know you're not safe? Come in and close the door."

"Where is Andy?" Meg cried.

Madame Doom's dark eyes grew wide. "Andy? I'm sorry. I don't know who you mean."

"We know he's in here," I said. "We heard him scream."

"You're supposed to be my Helper," Meg said. She shoved the Helper card in Madame Doom's face. "Where is Andy?"

"Andy? Hey — Andy?" Sam shouted.

"In back," I said. I led the way. I brushed past Madame Doom and pushed through the beaded curtain. It clattered loudly as the five of us burst through.

Into a small, dimly lit back room.

"Andy?" I called. And then I froze.

And stared at the most horrifying thing I had ever seen.

Andy. Sprawled facedown over a table. Arms dangling to the floor.

Not moving. Not moving.

An arrow sticking straight up from the middle of his back.

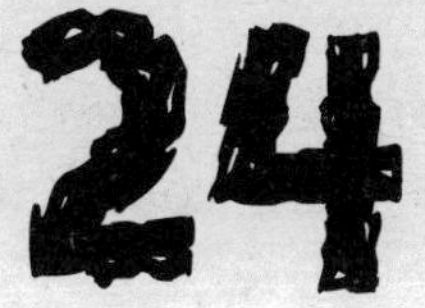

I let out a gasp. My knees started to fold, and I nearly fell.

Meg opened her mouth in a scream of horror. Marco went pale. He and Sam staggered back to the wall.

We all gaped at Andy, sprawled limply over the table.

Madame Doom stepped through the beaded curtain. She had an ugly grin on her face.

I cried out when I saw what was in her hands. A crossbow.

"Who says women aren't good hunters?" she cried in her booming, deep voice. "Which one of you will be next?"

Meg, Jessica, and I backed up to the wall. My heart pounded so hard it hurt. I could feel the blood pulsing at my temples.

And then I let out a scream of shock *as Andy sat up.*

He sat straight up and shook his head. He raised his dark eyes to Madame Doom.

"I . . . can't do this," Andy said.

"Andy? You — you're *alive*?" Meg stammered.

Andy turned to us. "I'm sorry, guys," he said. "I didn't want to scare you. But Madame Doom made me do it."

Madame Doom's grin faded. She lowered the crossbow. "Boy, you've made a big mistake," she told Andy. "Better shut up."

"I don't care!" Andy shouted. "I can't do that to these guys. They're my friends."

He reached behind him and pulled the arrow from his back. "It's a fake," he said. "It's a total fake." He tossed the arrow on the floor.

Madame Doom stepped heavily toward Andy. "Maybe you want to think about what you're saying, young man? You *do* want to go home sometime?"

Andy ignored her threat. He jumped to his feet. "She told me to pretend to be dead. Shot in the back. She said she wanted to make the game scarier."

"I . . . I sure believed it," I said. "I almost fainted."

"I'm sorry," Andy said. "She promised me if I did it, she would give me a little Horror and send me home right away."

He sighed. "I really want to go home. But I

couldn't go through with it. I couldn't do that to you guys."

"Very touching," Madame Doom said sarcastically. "But I've got news for you, sonny. The hunt is real — and it's still on."

She raised the crossbow and aimed at me.

"No!" I cried. I raised my hands to shield my face.

"But you're supposed to be my Helper!" Meg screamed.

Madame Doom tossed back her head, and an ugly laugh escaped her throat. "You kids are slow as snails. You haven't caught on yet? Chiller didn't give you Helper cards — he gave you *Hunter* cards! I'm a Hunter!"

Her words sent a chill down my back. I thought of Chef Belcher . . . Murder the Clown . . . the arrows flying at us in the darkness. Yes. Yes. They only *pretended* to be helping. They were the Hunters. We couldn't see them — but they were the ones sending the arrows flying at us.

I pictured the crossbow lying on the ground near Murder the Clown's feet. He lied. He lied to us about the Hunter running away. Murder was the Hunter.

Why didn't I figure it out?

Now we were trapped here. Like targets in a shooting gallery.

I knew I couldn't just stand there. I ducked my head — and took off.

I darted past Madame Doom. The beaded curtain clattered as I pushed through it.

"Stop!" she shouted. She burst through the curtain with the crossbow raised.

I gazed around frantically. Suddenly, I had an idea.

I grabbed her crystal ball off its pedestal. I pulled my arm back — and I heaved the shimmering ball at her stomach.

"No!" she screeched. "Not my crystal ball!"

She dropped the crossbow. The crystal ball bounced off her stomach and she dove for it before it hit the floor.

I pulled the front door open and tore out of there. The other five kids were right behind me.

We ran across the empty plaza, in and out of dim pools of light. Our shoes thudded loudly on the pavement. The only other sounds were the shrill screams pouring out of the Tunnel of Screams.

The screams rang in my ears as I ran. I glanced back once, to see if Madame Doom was chasing after us. But the plaza was empty.

I led the way around the side of a small restaurant called Weasel Burger. A blinking sign read: SUPERSIZE YOUR WEASEL BURGER FOR $1 MORE.

I wasn't in the mood for HorrorLand jokes. I was frightened and tired and frantic to get out of this game and go home.

We stopped at the back of the restaurant. *Yuccck.* A long garbage dumpster smelled like it held weasel meat that had gone bad a week ago.

I held my breath. We ducked behind it just in case someone came by.

I leaned my back against the dumpster and struggled to catch my breath.

I turned to see if everyone else was okay. We all looked pale in the dim light from the back of the restaurant. Pale and frightened.

"What are we going to do now?" Marco asked. "There aren't any little Horrors to take us home. And there are no Helpers. The game is a total cheat."

"Chiller lied," Jessica said. "He doesn't want us to escape. He wants to keep us here for the Hunters to get us."

"Maybe we just wait till tomorrow," Sam said. "When the gate opens and visitors come. We can find someone to help us."

"Where can we wait?" Meg asked, peeking around the side of the dumpster. "The Hunters will be after us. They'll find us. We won't *survive* till the park opens tomorrow."

I heard running footsteps.

I froze as three figures came charging toward us. As they came closer, I saw their black-and-orange uniforms.

Horror guards.

"You kids — stop right there!" one of them boomed. "Freeze. Don't move."

25

The guards were tall and powerful looking. Their dark eyes locked angrily on us. They had sharp horns that poked out of the sides of their black uniform caps.

I pressed my back against the dumpster as they closed in on us.

"Don't anyone move!" the biggest guard ordered. He had a gold badge on his chest. The two others had silver badges.

"You're in a world of trouble." His voice echoed over the empty plaza. "Freeze right there. I won't say it again."

"The park is closed," a Silver Badge said, eyeing us one by one. "Couldn't you tell?"

"What are you doing here after closing?" the other Silver Badge demanded.

They stood stiffly, hands at their waists. As if expecting a fight.

"We — we're playing a game," Marco stammered.

"A game?" the big guard shouted. "What kind of a game?"

"It's hard to explain," I said.

"No one is allowed in the park after closing," a Silver Badge said. "There are no games after closing."

"Did someone dare you to stay in the park all night?" Gold Badge demanded.

"Is that the game?" a guard asked. "That's a dangerous game. Is that what's going on here?"

Suddenly, an exciting thought ran through my mind: *Maybe these guards can help us. Maybe they can get us OUT of here.*

I took a step forward. "We . . . we're sorry," I said. "We know we shouldn't be here. If you take us to the exit, we'll leave. We won't come back. Promise."

The other kids caught on quickly.

"Yes. Help us find the exit."

"Let us out and we'll hurry home."

The three guards stared hard at us. Then they put their heads together and began chattering, too low for us to hear.

My heart began to pound. I didn't dare take a breath.

Would they do it? Would they guide us out of the park and away from Jonathan Chiller and his crazy game?

Finally, Gold Badge turned back to us. Again,

he eyed us one by one. He had a menacing scowl on his face.

"Okay," he said. "Follow me."

My heart skipped a beat. I wanted to jump up and down and let out a cheer.

"You're taking us to the exit?" I said.

Gold Badge nodded. "Yes. We're going to let you go."

He led the way. The two silver badges followed. My new friends and I followed behind them.

We all tried to hide our excitement. We kept our smiles to ourselves.

Once we were out in the parking lot, we could celebrate our victory over Jonathan Chiller.

The Horror guards led us away from the plaza. We walked along the side of Stagger Inn, the big hotel. I could see the main HorrorLand exit gate straight ahead.

As we walked closer, I saw that the gate was closed and padlocked.

The guards stopped and studied the lock. Gold Badge reached into his uniform pants pocket. "I have the gate key," he said.

Yesssss! I thought. I felt so happy, I thought I might explode.

The guard raised a long, silvery key. He lowered it to the padlock on the gate.

All six of us had our eyes straight ahead on that lock. We didn't breathe. We didn't say a word.

I knew we were all thinking the same thing: *Let us out. Let us out. Let us out.*

The guard pulled the key away from the lock. He turned to us. "Oh, wait," he said. "I have one question for you."

We stared at him in silence. I didn't take my eyes from the key.

He had started to slip it into the lock — then he stopped. What question made him stop?

"Where are your parents?" he asked.

No one spoke. Sam and I exchanged glances.

Why did he ask that question? Was he saying he wouldn't let us out of the park unless our parents were nearby waiting for us?

"They're . . . in the parking lot," I said. It was the first thing that popped into my head.

"Yeah," Jessica chimed in. "Waiting for us. In the parking lot."

The three guards studied us. "Let's see," Gold Badge said.

He peered through the exit gate. I could see the lighted parking lot on the other side.

"The lot is empty," he said. "I don't see anyone waiting for you out there."

I let out a sigh. I wished I'd thought of a better lie.

"Let us out," Meg said. "We'll find our parents once we're out of here."

Gold Badge shook his head. "No can do," he said.

"Why?"

"What do you mean?"

"You won't let us go?"

We surrounded him, all shooting questions at him at once.

He slid the silver key back into his uniform pocket. He shook his head, saying *no* to all of our questions.

I had a heavy, sinking feeling in my stomach. I wanted to grab the key from his pocket and unlock the gate myself.

"Back off, kids," one of the other guards barked.

"I can't let you go off on your own," Gold Badge said. "I can't release you without your parents."

"But our parents are expecting us at home," I said. "If you let us go —"

"Where is home?" he demanded.

I didn't answer. If I told him home was a few hundred miles from here, I knew I'd never get out. And I'd never be able to explain.

None of us could.

"Let's go. Follow us," a guard ordered.

"Where are you taking us?" Jessica demanded.

"To the security office," he said. "We'll wait there till we can locate your parents."

Should we tell them about Jonathan Chiller? About the game he was forcing us to play?

I thought about it as the three Horrors marched us away from the exit gate.

Maybe we should stay away from Chiller House. Maybe the old man is waiting there with all of his Hunters, crossbows ready.

If we tell the guards about Chiller's crazy game, will they believe us?

Why should they?

I decided not to say a word about Chiller. I studied the faces of my friends. I could see they were thinking the same thing.

"We're never getting out of here," Sam muttered as we walked. He shook his head. "We came so close to escaping. . . ."

I shivered. It had to be after midnight, and the late-night air was cold and damp.

The guards were herding us along the backs of the plaza shops. It was dark back here. The shops were all closed and empty, no light from their windows.

"Are your parents staying at the Stagger Inn?" one of the guards asked.

"Uh . . . not exactly," I said.

He stepped in front of us. It was so dark, we nearly bumped into him.

"Not exactly?" he boomed. "What does that mean? Yes or no?"

"No," I answered.

"Well, where are you kids staying?" he demanded.

I couldn't think of a good lie.

"Nowhere," Jessica spoke up. "We just got here today. We're not really staying anyplace."

At least she was telling the truth.

"Is that why you're wandering the park at all hours?" Gold Badge demanded.

"Uh . . . not really," I said again.

The guards motioned us forward. We continued walking along the backs of the shops.

My brain was spinning. *We have no choice*, I thought. *We're going to have to tell them the truth.*

We stepped into a square of pale light. I turned and saw where we were.

We were behind Chiller House. The light was on in the back room.

I peered in through the window — and gasped.

"I don't believe this," I muttered.

I'd seen something that could change everything.

27

Madame Doom was sitting on a stool in front of a dressing table. She had her back turned. But I could see her face clearly as she gazed into the dressing room mirror.

As I watched, she pulled off her long black hair. A wig.

Underneath the wig, she had thinning white hair pulled straight back off a wide forehead. She picked up a sponge and began wiping the color off her cheeks.

"What's up with this?" I murmured.

And that's when I recognized the face in the mirror.

Jonathan Chiller!

Sam bumped my shoulder and pointed to a side of the window. And I saw a clown costume hanging on a peg. A clown mask with an ax attached to the top.

Beside that, a chef's apron and hat. A mirrored face mask. A magician's top hat. Other costumes.

"Oh, wow!" I exclaimed. I stood up straight.

"What's wrong with you kids?" a guard asked sternly. "Let's get moving now."

We ignored him. We were all staring in shock through the back window of Chiller House.

And for the first time, we all knew the truth.

Jonathan Chiller was also Chef Belcher, Madame Doom, Murder the Clown, and all the others.

Jonathan Chiller played every character.

There was only one enemy — one Hunter. That old man sitting in front of the mirror.

"Look — on that shelf!" Marco cried.

Yes. On a shelf above the mirror — six little red chests.

I turned to the others. "Everything Chiller does is a total fake," I said. "He made us think all those people were hunting us. But it was only him."

"We outnumber the old man six to one," Marco said. "Let's go get him and collect those Horrors."

"Only one little problem," I said. I motioned to the three guards.

"I don't know what you kids are jabbering about," Gold Badge said, stepping toward us. "And I don't really care. You're in a world of trouble."

"Trespassing in the park after closing hours," one of his partners said.

"You kids should stop talking among yourselves and start thinking about telling us the truth," the leader said. "Now, let's move. To the security office."

We took a step or two. Then stopped as a high-pitched voice rang out from down the long row of shops.

"Help me! Somebody!"

Everyone froze. The voice was shrill and frightened.

"Help! Help me! I need help! Anybody! HELP ME!"

28

The cries seemed to freeze in the air.

The voice was so terrified, I felt a cold shudder run down my body.

The three Horror guards took off running, moving heavily along the backs of the shops.

"This is our chance," Jessica said. "Move!"

The guards disappeared into the thick blackness. We started to run along the side of Chiller House toward the front.

I ran next to Jessica. She couldn't hide the smile on her face.

"That was *you* — wasn't it?" I said. "You did that voice crying for help?"

She nodded. Her smile grew wider. "My dad is a ventriloquist. He taught me how to throw my voice."

"You totally fooled those guards," I said.

We reached the front of the store. Andy lowered his shoulder and pushed the front door open.

The bell above the door clanged loudly as the six of us burst into the front aisle. Chiller came walking out from the back room.

He wore a dark brown bathrobe and bedroom slippers. He blinked and his eyes went wide. He was definitely surprised to see us all there.

"Get out of here," he said softly, calmly. "The Hunters will be here soon. You will be sitting ducks."

"Nice try," I said. "But we know your secret."

"We know you're all alone."

"No, I'm not," Chiller insisted. He raised his eyes to the door.

It swung open and the three guards rushed in. They scowled angrily at us.

"Sorry about this, Mr. Chiller," the leader said. "They tricked us."

"Tell you what," Chiller told the guards. "Take them to the Bottomless Barbecue Pit and drop them in. Bring them back when they are crispy on the outside and medium well done — okay?"

"No problem," the guard said. He turned to us. "Okay, Roast Meat — let's move."

29

I gasped as the guards moved toward us.

"You're really going to *barbecue* us?" Jessica cried.

Chiller laughed. "No. I'm joking. I admit it. I have a sick sense of humor."

He waved the guards back. "Thanks for your help. But you three can leave," he said. "I can handle these kids on my own. They are my special guests. I'll see that they get home safely."

The guards frowned and shook their heads. Grumbling to themselves, they turned and disappeared out the front door.

Chiller stood beside the counter, a tense smile on his face. He still had a smear of Madame Doom's makeup on one cheek. "Well, well," he murmured. "Here we are."

I took a few steps toward him. "We saw the red chests in your back room," I said. "Give us the little Horrors and send us home."

Chiller's smile faded. "No, I shall not," he said. "You haven't won the game."

"Yes, we have," I insisted. "We know your secret. We know you are all alone."

"We know you played all the Hunters," Marco said, stepping up beside me.

Chiller's eyes narrowed behind his old-fashioned square glasses. He stared at us coldly. His mouth turned down in an angry scowl.

Marco and I took a step back. I didn't like the menacing expression on the old man's face. What did he plan to do?

To my surprise, he let out a loud sob.

His stern expression fell apart. His whole face appeared to droop.

"Of *course* I'm all alone," he wailed. "I wasn't allowed to have friends. I had to stay in my room and create my *own* world. I had to create my *own* friends."

He slammed his fist down on the counter. "The only way I can have friends is if I play them *myself*!"

He lowered his head. He stood there muttering to himself.

I turned to the other kids. Everyone looked surprised. Confused.

"Are you going to let us go home now?" I asked Chiller.

He just kept muttering to himself. I don't know

if he even heard me. He had his head down. It was like he was in his own world.

"We can rush right past him," Jessica whispered. "We can make a run for the back room. Grab those chests. Pull out the little Horrors and let them take us home."

"Yes. Let's do it," Marco said.

Chiller hadn't moved. Did he hear what we planned to do?

I motioned everyone forward. Walking quickly, we started down the aisle toward the back room.

We didn't get far.

Suddenly, Chiller pulled himself up straight. He stepped away from the counter. I guess he'd been listening the whole time.

"This is still my game," he said. "And guess what. I don't like to lose!"

He moved to block the door to the back room. "I'm a hunter! I'm a real hunter!" Chiller screamed at the top of his lungs. "You are my prey. You will not get away!"

We froze and stared at him as he screamed. What was our next move? What could we do?

To my surprise, Meg pulled something off a display shelf. Then she dropped to her knees on the floor. I squinted into the light and saw that she had two space alien figures in her hands.

She stood them on their legs. She made them face each other. She moved their metal arms up and down.

What is she doing? I wondered. *Has she totally lost her mind?*

"What do you think you are doing?" Chiller demanded angrily. He took several heavy steps toward Meg.

"Can you show me how these work?" Meg asked. "These space aliens are pretty awesome."

Chiller stared at her. I could see he was thinking hard.

Meg moved the two figures on the floor. "How do you make this one move its head?" she asked Chiller. "Do they come with weapons?"

Marco picked up a small robot figure and dropped next to Meg on the floor. "I'm totally into comic superheroes," he said. "This looks like a Bot villain from The Ooze."

He moved his robot toward Meg's two aliens.

I had my eyes on Chiller. Now I knew what Meg and Marco were trying to do. But would Chiller really fall for such a cornball trick?

Jessica quickly joined in. She picked up three more Bots from the table. "We can have a war," she told Meg and Marco. She sat down beside them. "Here. Line up your figures."

Meg turned to Chiller again. "Will you show us how to work these?"

No way will this work, I thought.

To my shock, a smile spread over Chiller's face. He walked over to Meg and the other two kids on the floor.

He squatted down and picked up one of Meg's alien figures. "The controls are inside the head," he told her. "Watch."

He pushed something on the alien's back, and the head snapped to one side. I saw a row of red and black buttons inside the alien's neck.

Chiller began to show them what the different buttons did.

I shook my head. Was he so desperate for friends that he really believed Meg, Marco, and Jessica were interested in his toys?

Meg's plan to distract Chiller seemed to be working. He was down on the floor with them.

I didn't hesitate another second. I motioned for Andy and Sam to follow me. Then the three of us took off, running to the back room.

As we thundered past, Chiller's eyes bulged in surprise. He stuck out a hand, trying to trip me.

But I jumped over his arm and kept running.

I reached the back room easily, with Andy and Sam close behind.

"Stop! Freeze!" Chiller shouted from the front. "Get out of there! That's private! Get *out*!"

But I dove to the shelf. I grabbed two of the little red chests. I tossed one to Sam. Andy grabbed two more.

"Get out of there!" Chiller shouted. I could hear him thudding toward us.

I pulled open the red chest. Reached inside.

Empty.

I turned. Andy and Sam held the lids open on their chests.

Empty. All empty.

Jonathan Chiller stepped into the doorway. He stood there blocking our way out.

He smiled a cold smile and quietly said two words.

"You lose."

Chiller stood there blocking our escape. He had beads of sweat on his balding head. His cheeks were red. He was breathing hard.

"Maybe I like to play games," he said. "And maybe you think I'm desperate for friends. But I'm not stupid."

He narrowed his eyes behind the square glasses. "But now I think we *know* who the stupid ones are. Did you really think you could escape so easily?"

"Y-you said it was a game," I stammered. "You said we could go home when it was over."

"I've got a few NEW games we could play," he said in his hoarse, croaky voice. "But I don't think you'll like them — because you're already LOSERS!"

"Let us go," I said. "Give us a break. We've been here all night. We don't want to play any more games."

That made him laugh. A sick, shrill laugh that sounded like a cough.

"You don't have a choice," he said. "Maybe we shall play the Shrink-A-Head game. Does that sound like fun?"

We stared back at him. No one answered.

"Did you know it's possible to shrink a head while it's still on a living body?" His tiny eyes flashed behind the glasses. He rubbed his hands together.

"You all have such perfectly lovely heads for shrinking. I can shrink them down to the size of a prune. Really, I can. It's so quick, too. Not exactly painless, but it's quick. Does anyone want to volunteer?"

Was Chiller serious?

In the front room, I could see the greenish-yellow shrunken heads dangling from the ceiling.

I searched desperately around the little room for a weapon I could use — anything that might get us out of there.

But there was nothing useful on the dressing table with all its makeup jars and bottles. Nothing useful among all the masks and costumes hanging on the wall.

Or *was* there?

A crazy idea popped into my head. Crazier than Meg picking up the toys and starting to play.

Friends . . . Chiller's friends . . .

Desperate for friends . . . Chiller wouldn't want to LOSE his friends . . . His friends . . .

Meg had tried a crazy trick. Now it was my turn.

I dove forward. I pulled the Murder the Clown mask off its hook. The ax bobbed on top of the mask. I slid the mask down over my face. I moved it till I could see out the eye holes.

"Hey — stop it! Put that down!" Chiller screamed.

I wrapped the red clown ruffle around my neck.

I motioned to Sam. He pulled Chef Belcher's hat onto his head. He tugged the chef's apron off its hook and began to wrap it around him.

Jessica pushed Chiller out of the doorway. She ran to the dressing table and pulled on the long black hair of Madame Doom's wig. She reached for Madame Doom's long purple scarf.

Meg slipped on Mondo the Magical's top hat. She reached for his tuxedo jacket.

"Stop it! Stop it!" Chiller wailed. His face turned bright red. His eyes bulged till it looked as if they could pop out of his head.

He made a grab for me. But I ducked away.

"You can't do this!" he cried. "Those are my friends! You can't! You can't!"

Wearing our costumes, we began to circle Chiller. And we began to repeat, over and over, in low voices: "Good-bye, Jonathan Chiller . . . Good-bye, Jonathan Chiller . . . Good-bye, Jonathan Chiller . . ."

He raised his hands in front of him as if to shield himself.

"No! Those are my friends!" he screamed over our chant. "My only friends! You can't do this!"

"Good-bye, Jonathan Chiller . . . Good-bye, Jonathan Chiller . . . Good-bye, Jonathan Chiller . . ." We circled him in costume.

He lowered his head and broke through our circle. He disappeared into the front of the store.

I heard a crash. He knocked a display over.

More running footsteps. He was still screaming. "You can't take my friends! You can't take my friends!"

I stood there in the Murder the Clown mask, breathing hard. I gazed at Chef Belcher and Madame Doom.

It was an insane idea. And it drove Jonathan Chiller crazy.

But what did he plan to do now?

31

We chased after him. I struggled to see through the eye holes of the rubber mask. The fake ax bobbed heavily on top of my head.

The chef hat was too big for Sam. It slipped down over his eyes. Meg had the same problem with the magician's top hat.

We followed Chiller to the front counter. He was fumbling around in a drawer.

When he stood up, he had a bunch of little green-and-purple Horrors in his hands. "Here," he cried. "Give me back my friends, and you can leave. . . ."

He waved the little Horror figures at us. "Go. Go home. You win. You found a way to win. Stealing my friends. I . . . I can't allow it."

"Are you — are you really going to send us home?" I stammered. "Or is this another one of your tricks?"

"Take off the costumes! Take them off!" he cried.

We scrambled out of the costumes. I tore off the clown mask and set it down on a table. Sam dropped the chef hat and apron on top of it.

Chiller began tossing the Horrors at us. We grabbed for them wildly.

Horrors bounced off the tables and rolled onto the floor. We scrambled until we each held one.

"Go ahead!" Chiller cried. "Go. Hold them in your hands — and GO!"

I didn't have to be asked twice. I did just as Chiller said.

"Good-bye, guys!" I called out. Then I wrapped my hands around the little Horror, shut my eyes tight, squeezed the Horror . . . squeezed it — and waited.

Waited to be carried home.

Waited.

Nothing happened.

And then I felt a sharp pull. I opened my eyes and gazed into a bright yellow-green light. The light seemed to pull me . . . draw me closer . . . pull me with a powerful force.

Swept up in a hurricane wind. I felt myself lifted up . . . lifted and pulled away. Until the light surrounded me, and I was part of a glowing fireball flying through space.

I landed on my bed in my own bedroom. Had I been holding my breath the whole time? I let it out in a long *whoosh*.

My eyes glanced over the football poster on my wall. The dirty clothes I'd left in a heap beside my bed. The underwater screen saver on my laptop.

Yes. Home. I heard a voice and turned to the doorway.

My big hulk of a brother was leaning there, staring at me. I have to admit it — I was never so glad to see him.

I jumped to my feet and started across the room. "Hey, Brandon — did you miss me?" I cried.

"Huh?" He squinted at me. "Miss you? Did you *go* somewhere?"

EPILOGUE

Jonathan Chiller had to work till all hours that night. The shop had to be put back together.

The action figures had to be organized and returned to their tables. During all the excitement, he had knocked over a display of human skull lunch boxes. It took a while to get that back up.

And then, of course, there were his friends. He had to be so careful with them. He had to hang the masks and the costumes and the props so carefully.

Madame Doom would look beautiful again with her long, flowing hair. The chef would be able to reign as king of his restaurant again. He made sure that all of his friends were okay.

Yes, he took good care of his friends.

By morning, Chiller House stood in its usual glowing splendor. Every rubber spider and cockroach, every shriveled shrunken head in place.

The sun came up big and golden and warmed the park. Bright enough to wash away any memories of a game gone bad.

And when the bell over the front door jingled, Chiller was ready to welcome the new customers. A new day and new customers.

A tall, dark-haired girl and her shy, copper-haired friend, both in tennis shorts and skater T-shirts. Gazing around at the wonders of the shop through their dark glasses.

"Welcome, and have a look around," he said. He waved to the shelves and tables of his collections. "See anything you like?" he asked them.

And then he gave them his warmest smile. *"Why don't you take a little Horror home with you?"*

JONATHAN CHILLER

OCCUPATION: Souvenir Shop Owner & Weird Person

HOBBY: Just "chillin'"

HOMETOWN: Chill-icothe, Ohio

COLLECTS: Scary items — skulls, shrunken heads, snake fangs, bat wings, and bad report cards

HORRORLAND SPLAT STATS

WEIRDNESS:

EXTREME WEIRDNESS:

HORRIFYING IDEAS:

HORRIFYING BREATH:

In HorrorLand, Chiller House is the place to go for joke gifts and funny souvenirs you'll never forget. You'll never forget them because they'll probably eat you, or shrink your head, or turn your skin into burning lava. Everyone knows Jonathan Chiller is a joker. He's so funny, he's a SCREAM.

Ready for more thrills and chills?

A terrifying new HorrorLand adventure begins next time — when you pay a visit to the Hall of Horrors.

Don't look for it on the HorrorLand map. Horror Hall is hidden in the darkest shadows of the park. It is the place for kids who have frightening stories to tell.

Mickey Coe will be the first to enter. His story is about a black cat. This black cat might be *very* unlucky for Mickey. He has a big question: Is the cat alive? Or has it come back from the dead to haunt him?

Can you guess why Goosebumps HorrorLand Hall of Horrors #1 is called *Claws*?

You'll find out when you enter. Go ahead. Don't be afraid. Step inside.

There's always room for one more SCREAM.

CLAWS!

About the Author

R.L. Stine's books are read all over the world. So far, his books have sold more than 300 million copies, making him one of the most popular children's authors in history. Besides Goosebumps, R.L. Stine has written the teen series Fear Street and the funny series Rotten School, as well as the Mostly Ghostly series, The Nightmare Room series, and the two-book thriller *Dangerous Girls*. R.L. Stine lives in New York with his wife, Jane, and Minnie, his King Charles spaniel. You can learn more about him at www.RLStine.com.